KNULP

by the same author

STEPPENWOLF

NARZISS AND GOLDMUND

SIDDARTHA

GERTRUDE

THE JOURNEY TO THE EAST

THE PRODIGY

DEMIAN

PETER CAMENZIND

THE GLASS BEAD GAME

ROSSHALDE

KLINGSOR'S LAST SUMMER

IF THE WAR GOES ON ...

POEMS

Knulp

THREE TALES FROM THE LIFE OF KNULP

HERMANN HESSE

TRANSLATED BY
RALPH MANHEIM

JONATHAN CAPE
THIRTY BEDFORD SQUARE LONDON

This translation first published in Great Britain 1972

Originally published in German under the title
KNULP: DREI GESCHICHTEN AUS DEM LEBEN KNULPS

Jonathan Cape Ltd, 30 Bedford Square, London WC1

ISBN Hardback 0 224 00720 3
Paperback 0 224 00729 7

Printed in Great Britain by
Lowe and Brydone (Printers) Ltd
on paper made by John Dickinson & Co. Ltd
Bound by James Burn & Co. Ltd, Esher, Surrey.

Contents

EARLY SPRING

3

MY RECOLLECTIONS OF KNULP

51

THE END

77

EARLY SPRING

Early Spring

ONCE, early in the nineties, our friend Knulp had to go to the hospital for several weeks. It was mid-February when he was discharged and the weather was abominable. After only a few days on the road, he felt feverish again and was obliged to think about getting a roof over his head. He had always had plenty of friends, he would have met with a friendly reception in almost every town in the region. But he was strangely proud about such things and any friend from whom he accepted help could take it as an honor.

This time he remembered Emil Rothfuss, the tanner in Lächstetten, and at nightfall, amid rain and west wind, he knocked at the tanner's door. Rothfuss opened the shutters a crack and shouted down into the dark street: "Who's there? Can't it wait until daylight?"

Tired as he was, Knulp perked up at the sound of his friend's voice. He remembered a little song he had made up years before when he and Rothfuss had been traveling companions for a month, and started to sing it:

A man walked into the hotel
After the day was done.
I know those tired features well,
It must be the Prodigal Son.

The tanner opened the shutters wide and leaned far out of the window.

"Knulp! Is it you, or is it your ghost?"

"It's me!" cried Knulp. "But you can come down the stairs, you don't have to jump out the window."

Happily the tanner ran down and opened the little front door. Knulp had to blink when his friend held the smoking oil lamp up to his face.

"And now, get inside!" Rothfuss cried out excitedly, drawing his friend into the house. "You can tell me all about it later. There's some supper left. And there's a bed for you too. Good God, what weather to be out in! Have you got decent shoes at least?"

Disregarding his questions and astonishment, Knulp stopped on the stairs to unfold his turned-up trouser cuffs, then climbed through the half light with assurance, though he had not set foot in the house for four years.

In the hallway outside the door to the big room, he hesitated. The tanner bade him go in, but Knulp took him by the hand and held him back.

"Hold on," he whispered. "It seems you're married now."

"That's right."

"Well, you see. Your wife doesn't know me. Maybe she won't be glad to see me. I wouldn't want to be in the way."

"Ho-ho! In the way!" Rothfuss laughed, opened the door wide, and pushed Knulp into the brightly lit room. Over the dining table a large oil lamp hung on three chains. A light cloud of tobacco smoke hovered in mid-air; thin wisps of smoke floated over to the hot lamp-chimney, where they whirled up swiftly and vanished. On the table lay a newspaper and a pouch full of tobacco. The tanner's young wife jumped up from the little sofa on the far side of the room with embarrassed, not quite genuine alacrity, as if she had been awakened from a nap and didn't want to show it. For a moment Knulp blinked at her as though dazed by the glare, then looked into her light-gray eyes and held out his hand with a polite compliment.

"Well," said the tanner. "Here she is. And this is Knulp, my friend Knulp that I've told you about. Naturally he'll stay with us, we'll give him the journeyman's bed. Luckily it's empty. But first we'll have a drink of cider together, and Knulp must have something to eat. Wasn't there some liver sausage left?"

The tanner's wife rushed out of the room and Knulp looked after her.

"She's kind of frightened," he said in an undertone. But Rothfuss wouldn't agree.

"No children yet?" Knulp asked.

At that point she came back, bringing the sausage on a pewter plate. She set it down beside the breadboard, on which she had placed half a loaf of bread with the cut side down. A carved inscription ran round the circular breadboard: Give us this day our daily bread.

"Lis, do you know what Knulp just asked me?"

"Forget it," said Knulp. And with a smile he turned to the lady of the house: "By your leave, ma'am."

But Rothfuss wouldn't forget it.

"If we had no children. That's what he asked me."

"Goodness!" she laughed, and left the room again.

"You haven't got any?" Knulp asked when she was gone.

"No, not yet. She's taking her time. It's better that way for the first few years. But dig in, and I hope you like it."

The tanner's wife brought in the gray and blue earthenware cider pitcher, set down three glasses, and filled them. Her movements were deft. Knulp watched her and smiled.

"Your health, old friend!" cried the tanner, holding out his glass. But Knulp was a gentleman. "Ladies first," he said. "Your health, ma'am. Prosit, old man!"

They clinked glasses and drank. Beaming with pleasure, Rothfuss winked at his wife and asked her if she had noticed what fine manners his friend had.

She had noticed from the start.

"Herr Knulp is more polite than you," she said. "He knows what's right and proper."

"Nonsense," said the guest. "We all do what we've learned. When it comes to manners, you could easily put me to shame. And how beautifully you set the table, like at the finest hotel!"

"Doesn't she!" said the tanner, and laughed. "But that too was learned."

"Really? Where? Was your father a hotelkeeper?"

"No, he's been dead for years. I hardly knew him. But I waited on table for several years at the Ox. Maybe you've heard of it?"

"The Ox? Why, that used to be the best inn in Lächstetten."

"It still is. Isn't it, Emil? Nearly all our guests were traveling salesmen and tourists."

"I believe you, ma'am. I'm sure you had a pleasant life and made good money. But a home of your own is even better."

After neatly removing the skin and setting it aside on his plate, he slowly and with visible relish spread the soft sausage on his bread. From time to time he took a swallow of the good yellow cider. The tanner looked on with respectful appreciation, as Knulp's slender, delicate hands went through the necessary motions so neatly and easily, and the lady of the house also took pleasure in watching him.

"I must say you don't look so good," the tanner remarked critically, and Knulp had to admit that he had not been well of late and had been in the hospital. But he passed over the unpleasant parts of his story. His friend asked him what he meant to do next and warmly offered to keep him as long as he liked. That was exactly what Knulp had expected and counted on, but as though smitten with bashfulness, he merely thanked him offhandedly and postponed the discussion of such matters.

"We can talk about that tomorrow or the day after," he said negligently. "Thank goodness the world isn't coming to an end. Anyway, I'll stay here a little while."

He disliked making plans or promises too much ahead. He felt uncomfortable unless the morrow was his to dispose of as he pleased.

"If I should really stay here a while," he said after a time, "you'll have to put me down as your journeyman."

"That's rich!" said the tanner with a laugh. "You my journeyman! Anyway, you're not a tanner!"

"That doesn't matter. Don't you see? Tanning means nothing to me. It's said to be a fine trade, but I have no talent for work. But it would look good in my roadbook. I'd be eligible for sick pay."

"Can I see your book?"

Knulp reached into the inside pocket of his almost new suit and took out his roadbook, neatly enfolded in an oilcloth case.

The tanner looked at it and laughed. "Spotless! It looks as if you'd left your mother only yesterday morning."

He studied the entries and official stamps and shook his head with profound admiration. "What splendid order! With you, everything has to be just right."

Keeping his roadbook in order was indeed one of Knulp's hobbies. In its dazzling perfection, his roadbook was a delightful fiction, a poem. Each of the officially accredited entries bore witness to a glorious station in an honest, laborious life. The only seemingly discordant feature was his restlessness, attested by frequent changes of residence. The life certified by this official passport was a product of Knulp's invention, and with infinite art he spun out the fragile thread of this pseudo-career. In reality, though he did little that was expressly prohibited, he carried on the illegal and disdained existence of a tramp. Of course, he would hardly have been so unmolested in his lovely fiction if the police had not been well disposed toward him. They respected the cheerful, entertaining young fellow for his superior intelligence and occasional earnestness, and as far as possible left him alone. He had seldom been arrested and never convicted of theft or mendicancy, and he had highly respected friends everywhere. Consequently, he was indulged by the authorities very much as a nice-looking cat is indulged in a household, and left free to carry on an untroubled, elegant, splendidly aristocratic and idle existence.

"But that's enough now," he said, taking back his papers. "You'd have been in bed long ago if I hadn't turned up." And, with a compliment to the lady of the house, he arose.

"Come along, Rothfuss, and show me my bed."

The tanner lighted him up the narrow stairway to the journeyman's room on the top floor. Against the wall stood an empty iron bedstead and a wooden bed that was made up.

"Would you like a hot-water bottle?" asked the tanner in a fatherly tone.

"Don't rub it in," said Knulp with a laugh. "Naturally a master tanner like you wouldn't need one, now that he has such a pretty little wife."

"Exactly," said Rothfuss with enthusiasm. "Here you are getting into a cold attic bed, and sometimes there's no bed at all and you have to sleep in the hay. When an honest craftsman like me has a house and business and a nice wife. If you'd only wanted to, you could have been a master craftsman long ago and be doing better than me."

Meanwhile Knulp had hurriedly undressed and crawled shivering between the cold sheets.

"Go on, go on," he said. "I'm comfortable and ready to listen."

"I meant it seriously, Knulp."

"So did I, Rothfuss. But you mustn't get the idea that marriage is your invention. Good night now."

Next day Knulp stayed in bed. He still felt rather weak, and in any case he would hardly have gone out of doors in such weather. In the morning when his friend dropped in, Knulp told him not to worry about him, just to bring him a dish of soup at lunchtime.

All day he lay quiet and content in the dim light of the attic room. The cold and weariness of the road seeped away from him and he basked in a feeling of sheltered warmth. He listened to the regular thudding of the rain against the roof and to the fitful gusts of the warm, soft wind. Now and then he dozed off for half an hour and occasionally, as long as it was light enough, he leafed through his traveling library—a few sheets of paper on which he had copied poems and sayings, a bundle of newspaper clippings, and a few pictures that hc had cut out of magazines. Among these he had two favorites, which were creased and worn from frequent handling. One was the actress Eleonora Duse, the other a sailboat at sea in a high wind.

From boyhood Knulp had felt drawn to the sea and the north country; several times he had made a start in that direction, and once had gone as far as Brunswick. But time and time again a strange anxiety and homesickness had driven this migrant, who was always on the move and could never settle down anywhere, back to South Germany by forced marches. His carefreeness seemed to leave him when he found himself in a place with a strange dialect and customs, where no one knew him and where it was hard for him to keep his legendary roadbook in order.

At noon the tanner brought him soup and bread. He entered the room quietly and spoke in a frightened whisper; he thought Knulp must be sick, for he himself had never lain abed in broad daylight since the days of his measles and chicken pox. Knulp, who was feeling fine, didn't bother to explain, but merely said he would be well and up the next day.

Late in the afternoon there was a knock at the door. Knulp was dozing and made no answer. The tanner's wife tiptoed in, removed the empty soup dish, and put a bowl of coffee in its place on the stool beside the bed.

Knulp had heard her come in, but whether because he felt lazy or merely out of caprice, he kept his eyes closed and gave no sign of being awake. Standing there with the empty dish in her hand, the young woman cast a glance at the sleeper, whose head lay on his arm in its blue-checkered shirtsleeve. Struck by his fine dark hair and the almost childlike beauty of his carefree face, she stood a while, looking at the handsome young fellow about whom her husband had told her such strange stories. She saw the bushy eyebrows on his clear, delicately modeled forehead, his thin brown cheeks, his fine red mouth and slender neck, and she liked what she saw. She thought of the days when, as a waitress at the Ox, a springtime fancy would come over her and she would let a handsome young stranger like this one make love to her.

Thoughtful and slightly aroused, she leaned forward a little to see his whole face. The tin spoon slid off the plate and fell to the floor, and what with the stillness and embarrassing intimacy of the place, she was scared to death.

Knulp opened his eyes slowly and unsuspectingly, as though he had been sound asleep. He turned toward her, shaded his eyes with his hand for a moment, and said with a smile: "Why, it's Frau Rothfuss! And she's brought me coffee. A nice bowl of hot coffee, the very thing I was dreaming about. Thank you, Frau Rothfuss. By the way, what time is it?"

"Four," she said quickly. "Now drink it while it's hot. I'll come back later for the bowl."

And out she ran as though she hadn't a moment to spare. Knulp looked after her and listened as she hastily descended the stairs. His eyes were thoughtful and he shook his head several times, then he let out a soft birdlike whistle and turned to his coffee.

But an hour before dark he began to feel bored. His health was restored, he was wonderfully rested, and he wanted company. Contentedly he got out of bed and dressed, crept down the dark stairs as quietly as a cat, and slipped out of the house unnoticed. A damp wind was still blowing from the southwest, but the rain had stopped and there were clear spaces between the clouds.

Sniffing at the air, Knulp sauntered down the darkened street and across the deserted marketplace. Then he stood in the open doorway of a blacksmith's shop, watched the apprentices cleaning up, and, while warming his hands over the dying forge fire, struck up a conversation with the journeymen. He inquired about various acquaintances in the town, about deaths and marriages. The master took him for a fellow blacksmith, for Knulp knew the language of every trade and the signs by which its practitioners recognize one another.

Meanwhile Frau Rothfuss was making her evening soup, fiddling with the iron rings of the little stove, and peeling potatoes. When she had finished and the soup was safely simmering on a low fire, she took the kitchen lamp, went into the big room, and stood before the mirror. In it she found what she had been looking for: a full face with fresh cheeks and bluish-gray eyes. Her hair didn't seem quite right, and with a touch or two of her nimble fingers she put it in order. Then she gave her hands, which she had washed only a moment before, another wipe on her apron, picked up the lamp, and went quickly up to the attic.

She knocked at the door of the journeyman's room,

first softly, then a little louder. When there was no answer, she set the lamp down on the floor and opened the door with both hands, very cautiously for fear it would creak. Then she entered on her tiptoes, took one step, and ran her hands over the stool by the bedside.

"Are you asleep?" she asked in a soft voice. And then again: "Are you asleep? I've come to clear away the coffee things."

When there was no sound, not so much as a breath, she stretched out her hand toward the bed, but quickly withdrew it with an eerie feeling, and went out for the lamp. Finding the room empty, the bed carefully made, and even the pillows and featherbed shaken out, she rushed back down to the kitchen in confusion, torn between fright and disappointment.

Half an hour later, when the tanner had come in to supper and she had already set the table, she began to worry. But she was afraid to tell her husband about her visit to the attic room. Just then the outer gate opened, soft steps passed over the paved corridor and up the winding stairs, and there stood Knulp. He took off his trim brown felt hat and wished them good evening.

"Great guns!" the tanner cried out in consternation. "Where have you been? He's sick and off he goes, running around in the night! You'll catch your death."

"Right you are," said Knulp. "I see I'm just on time, Frau Rothfuss. I smelled your fine soup way over at the marketplace. That will keep my death away from me."

They sat down to eat. The master of the house was [illegible]ing talkative, he sang the praises of his home life and the advantages of being a master craftsman. He teased his guest and then lectured him in earnest; it was high time that he stopped gadding about doing nothing. Knulp listened but said little in reply, and the tanner's wife didn't open her mouth. She was annoyed with her husband, who struck her as uncouth compared to the handsome and well-mannered Knulp, and she showed her good opinion of the guest by the attentiveness with which she waited on him. At the stroke of ten, Knulp said good night and asked the tanner to lend him his razor.

"Did you ever see anybody so clean!" Rothfuss exclaimed. "The second his chin starts to tickle, his beard has to come off. Well, good night. I hope you feel better!"

Before going to his room, Knulp leaned out of the little window at the head of the stairs to take a look at the weather and see what was going on in the neighborhood. The wind had died down and between the roofs there was a black patch of sky studded with clear, damply shimmering stars.

He was about to pull in his head and close the window when suddenly the little window across from him, in the house next door, lighted up. He saw a small, low room very much like his own; a young servant girl had come in, holding a brass candlestick in one hand and in the other a large water pitcher, which she set down on the floor. Then she held the candle over her narrow bed. Covered with a coarse red blanket, it was plain but neat, and invited sleep. She put the candlestick down, he could not see where, and seated herself on a low green-painted wooden box, the typical servant girl's trunk.

The moment this unexpected scene began to unfold, Knulp had blown out his own candle, so as to avoid being seen, and now he stood quietly peering out of his window.

The girl across the way was the kind that appealed to him. She may have been eighteen or nineteen, not very tall, with an attractive olive complexion, brown eyes, and thick brown hair. Her pleasant, quiet face did not look exactly happy; all in all, she seemed rather woebegone as she sat there on her hard green box, and Knulp, who knew the world and young girls as well, had a pretty fair idea that the poor thing hadn't left her native village very long ago with her box, and was homesick. Holding her thin, dark-skinned hands in her lap, she sought brief comfort in sitting for a little while on her meager possessions and thinking of home.

As motionless in his window as she was in her room, Knulp peered with strange eagerness into this unknown human life, so innocently nursing its sweet sorrow in the candlelight without a thought that someone might be watching. He saw her kindly brown eyes, now unconcealed, now covered by long lashes, he saw the red light playing softly over her dark, childlike cheeks, and as he watched her slender young hands on the dark-blue cotton of her lap, he knew they were tired and resting awhile before getting down to undressing—the day's last chore.

At last the girl raised her head with its heavy pinned-up braids, heaved a sigh, looked dreamily but no less sorrowfully out into the void, and then bent down to untie her shoelaces.

Knulp was reluctant to leave his post, but it struck him as wrong and almost cruel to watch the poor child undressing. He would have liked to call out to her and chat with her a while, to make some joke that would send her to bed a little happier. But he was afraid she would take fright and blow out her candle if he called to her.

Instead, he resorted to one of his many arts. He began to whistle. The sound was so faint that it seemed to come from the distance. He whistled the folk song "In a cool green valley, a mill wheel turns all day," and he managed to make his whistling so frail and delicate that the girl listened for some time without knowing quite what it was. It was only at the third stanza that she slowly stood up and went to the window.

She leaned out and listened, while Knulp went on whistling. For a few measures she wagged her head in time with the tune. Then suddenly she looked up and saw where it came from.

"Is there somebody over there?" she asked in a whisper.

"Only a tanner's apprentice," he answered just as softly. "I didn't mean to prevent you from sleeping. I was a little homesick, so I thought I'd whistle a tune. But I also know some cheerful ones. —Are you a stranger here too?"

"I'm from the Black Forest."

"Ah, from the Black Forest. So am I. How do you like it here in Lächstetten? I don't like it at all."

"Oh, I don't know yet, I've only been here a week. But I don't really like it much. Have you been here long?"

"No, only three days. What village are you from?"

"You wouldn't know it."

"You never can tell. Or is it a secret?"

"Achthausen. It's only a hamlet."

"But a pretty one. The first thing you see is a chapel. Then there's a mill, a sawmill I think it is, and they've got a big yellow St. Bernard. Am I right or wrong?"

"My goodness, that's Bello!"

When she saw that he knew her village and had actually been there, the greater part of her suspicion left her; she perked up and asked eagerly: "Do you know Andres Flick?"

"No, I don't know anybody there. That's your father, isn't it?"

"Yes."

"Then you must be Fräulein Flick, and when I find out your first name I'll be able to write you a postcard the next time I pass through Achthausen."

"Do you want to leave here so soon?"

"No, I don't want to. But I want to know your name, Fräulein Flick."

"But I don't know yours either."

"I'm sorry about that, but it's easily mended. My name is Karl Eberhard. Now if we meet in the daytime you know what to call me, but what am I to call you?"

"Barbara."

"Thanks. That's fine. But it's a hard name to pronounce and I'm almost willing to bet they called you Bärbele at home."

"Yes, they did. But if you know everything, why do you ask so many questions? And now it's time to go to sleep. Good night, tanner."

"Good night, Fräulein Bärbele. Sleep well, and just because it's you, I'll whistle another tune. Don't run away, there's no charge."

He started right in and whistled a flamboyant yodel-like tune full of trills and turns, which leapt and sparkled like dance music. Amazed at his skill, she listened to the end. When he had done, she slowly drew the shutters tight and fastened them, while Knulp found his way to his room in the dark.

Next morning Knulp got up early and made use of the tanner's razor. But the tanner had worn a full beard for years and the razor was so neglected that Knulp had to hone it on his suspenders for half an hour before it would cut. When he had finished, he put on his coat, picked up his shoes, and went down to the kitchen, where it was warm and already smelled of coffee.

He asked the tanner's wife for a brush and polish for his shoes.

"Go 'long!" she cried. "That's not the kind of work for a man. Let me do it."

But that he would not allow, and when finally with an awkward laugh she set down the brush and polish before him, he did the work thoroughly, neatly, and with playful ease, like a man who did manual labor only very occasionally, when in the mood, but then cheerfully and with great care.

"Beautiful!" said the tanner's wife admiringly, and looked at him. "As shiny as if you were going to see your sweetheart."

"Oh, I wish I were."

"I believe you. I'll bet you've got a pretty one." She laughed again insinuatingly. "Maybe more than one?"

"Oh, that wouldn't be nice," said Knulp reproachfully. "I can show you a picture of her."

She stepped eagerly closer as he drew his oilcloth portfolio from his pocket and took out the picture of Duse. She studied it with interest.

"She's high-class," she began cautiously. "Almost like a real lady. But kind of skinny. Is her health all right?"

"Oh yes, as far as I know. But now I'll go say hello to the old man. I can hear him in the big room."

He went into the room and bade the tanner good morning. The room had been swept and looked friendly and homelike with its light-colored paneling, its clock, its mirror, and the photographs on the wall. A cozy room like this, thought Knulp, isn't bad in the winter, but it's not really worth marrying for. The favor shown him by the tanner's wife gave him no pleasure at all.

When they had had their coffee he went out in back with Rothfuss, who showed him through the tannery. Knulp knew almost every trade and amazed his friend by his knowledgeable questions.

"How do you know all that?" he asked with animation. "Anyone would think you were a journeyman tanner, or at least that you'd been one."

"A traveling man learns all sorts of things," said Knulp modestly. "Come to think of it, I learned about tanning from you. Don't you remember? Six or seven years ago, when we were on the road together. I made you tell me all about it."

"And you still remember all that?"

"Some of it, Rothfuss. But I won't take up any more of your time. Too bad, I'd have liked to give you a hand, but it's so damp and stuffy down there, and I've still got this cough. Goodbye for now, old man, I'll take a little turn in town while the rain holds off."

And neatly brushed, his brown felt hat tilted back just a little, he sauntered off with a light, jaunty step, carefully skirting the puddles. Rothfuss stood in the doorway looking after him.

"Lucky man," the tanner reflected with a twinge of envy. And on his way to the tanning pits Rothfuss thought about his eccentric friend who wanted nothing of life but to look on, and the tanner could not have said whether this was asking too much or too little. A man who worked hard and got ahead was better off in many ways, but he could never have such delicate, graceful hands or walk with so light and jaunty a step. No, Knulp was right in doing what his nature demanded and what few others could do, in speaking to strangers like a child and winning their hearts, in saying pleasant things to ladies of all ages, and making Sundays out of weekdays. You could only take him as he was, and when he needed a roof over his head, it was a pleasure and an honor to give him one; indeed, you almost wanted to thank him, for he brought lightness and gaiety into the house.

Meanwhile his guest, happy and alert with curiosity, strolled through the town, whistling a military march through his teeth, and, taking his time about it, sought out the places and people he knew from former days. First he climbed a steep hill to an outlying slum where he knew an unfortunate tailor, Schlotterbeck by name, who was forever mending old trousers and was seldom given a new suit to make. A great pity, for he was skilled at his trade, he had started out with high hopes and worked in good shops. But he had married young, he already had several children, and his wife had little talent for housekeeping.

Knulp found the tailor on the third floor of a house set back from the street. His little workshop hung like a bird's nest over the void, for the house was built on the hillside, and when you looked down from the windows, you not only had the three stories below you but further on a steep slope covered with pathetic slanting gardens and patches of grass and ending in a gray confusion of chicken coops, rabbit hutches, and woodsheds; the nearest roofs that could be seen lay far below, at the bottom of the valley. However, the workshop was light and airy, and as he sat cross-legged on his big table by the window the tailor could look out over the world like a lighthouse keeper.

"Morning, Schlotterbeck," said Knulp, stepping into the room. Blinded by the bright light, the tailor narrowed his eyes and peered in the direction of the door.

"Ah, Knulp!" he cried joyfully and held out his hand. "Back in town? And what's wrong, to bring you all the way up here?"

Knulp pulled up a three-legged stool and sat down. "Give me a needle and a bit of your very best brown wool, I want to check my equipment."

He removed his coat and vest, selected his yarn, threaded a needle, and with vigilant eyes inspected his whole suit, which still looked as good as new. Whenever he discovered a thin spot, a loose trimming, or a button that was not quite tight, he set it to rights with nimble fingers.

"And how are you otherwise?" Schlotterbeck asked. "The weather hasn't been so good. But then if a man has his health and no family . . ."

Knulp cleared his throat argumentatively.

"Yes, of course," he said wearily. "The Lord sends down His rain on righteous and unrighteous alike, and only the tailors keep dry. But you're never satisfied, are you, Schlotterbeck?"

"Oh, Knulp. I'm not complaining. But listen to the children screaming in there. There are five of them now. Here I sit, working my fingers to the bone till late at night, and it's never enough. And all you do is gad about."

"Wrong, my friend. I was in the hospital for four or five weeks in Neustadt, and they don't keep a man a minute longer than he absolutely needs, and nobody'd stay any longer anyway. The ways of the Lord are strange, friend Schlotterbeck."

"Keep your pious sayings to yourself."

"Lost your religion, eh? I've just been trying to get religion and that's why I came to see you. I want you to tell me all about it."

"Don't bother me with religion! In the hospital, you say? I'm sorry to hear that."

"Never mind, it's over now. I want you to tell me about Ecclesiasticus and Revelation. You see, I had plenty of time in the hospital, and they had a Bible. I read nearly all of it, so now I can put in a word too. A curious book, the Bible."

"You've got something there. It's curious, all right. Half of it must be lies, because nothing fits together. Maybe you understand it better, because you went to Latin school."

"I don't remember much of that."

"You see, Knulp . . ." The tailor spat through the open window and stared. There was bitterness in his face. "Religion is no good. It's no good and I'm through with it. Through with it."

The vagrant looked at him thoughtfully. "Really? Aren't you going too far, old friend? It seems to me there are some very good things in the Bible."

"Sure. And when you read a little further you always find the opposite. No, I'm fed up with it. Fed up."

Knulp had risen and picked up an iron.

"You could put a few chunks of coal on the fire," he suggested.

"What for?"

"I'd like to iron my vest a little, and it won't do my hat any harm either, after all that rain."

"Still the same old dandy!" cried Schlotterbeck with a note of irritation. "What's the good of dressing like a duke when you're half starved?"

Knulp smiled serenely. "It looks better and it gives me pleasure, and if you don't want to do it out of piety, just do it to be nice and to please an old friend."

The tailor left the room and soon came back with a hot iron.

"That's fine," said Knulp. "Thank you."

Cautiously he began to smooth the brim of his hat. But he was not as skillful at ironing as he was at sewing; his friend took the iron out of his hand and did it himself.

"That's very kind of you," said Knulp. "Now it's a Sunday hat again. But look here, tailor, you ask too much of the Bible. The way I see it, everybody's got to figure out for himself what's true and what life is like; those are things that you can't learn from any book. The Bible is old; in those days people didn't know a good many things that we know today; but for that very reason there are a lot of fine things in it, and true things too. Parts of it, I thought, were like a beautiful picture book. The way that girl—Ruth—goes through the fields gleaning, that's beautiful, you can smell the warm summer in it, or the way the Saviour sits down with the little children and thinks: You mean a lot more to me than all those grownups with their pride! If you ask me, he was right, and we can learn from him."

"Yes," Schlotterbeck admitted, "that's a fact. But it's easier to do that with other people's children than to have five of your own and not know how you're going to feed them."

He relapsed into bitter gloom and Knulp couldn't bear to see him that way. He resolved that before leaving he would say something to cheer him up. He thought a little while, then he leaned toward the tailor, looked earnestly into his face with his bright eyes, and said softly: "But don't you love your children?"

The tailor stared at Knulp in horror. "Of course I do! How can you say such a thing? Of course I love them, especially the oldest."

Knulp nodded earnestly.

"I'm going now, Schlotterbeck, and many thanks. My vest is worth twice as much now. —But you've got to be kindly and cheerful with your children, that's food and drink to them. And now listen, I'm going to tell you something that nobody knows and that you needn't repeat."

Mollified, the tailor looked attentively into Knulp's clear blue eyes, which had grown grave. Knulp spoke so softly that the tailor had difficulty in understanding him.

"Look at me! You envy me. You think: he has no family and no worries. But you're all wrong. I have a child, a little fellow two years old. He was taken in by strangers because his father was unknown and his mother died in childbed. There's no need for you to know what city he's in, but I know, and when I go there I creep up to the house. I stand by the fence and wait, and when I'm in luck I see the little fellow. But I can't hold out my hand to him or give him a kiss; the most I can ever do is whistle a tune for him as I go by. —Well, that's how it is, goodbye now, and be glad you have children."

Knulp continued on his way through the town. He stood for a while chatting at the window of a turner's shop and watched the swift play of the curly wood shavings. Farther on he stopped to say hello to the constable, who was devoted to him and held out his birchwood snuffbox. Wherever he went, old friends related the lesser and greater incidents of family and workshop, he heard of the untimely death of the municipal accountant's wife and of how the mayor's son had been misbehaving, and in return he reported on events in other towns, taking pleasure in the tenuous, good-humored ties which he, as friend, acquaintance, and sharer of secrets, had formed here and there with the more settled members of the population. It was Saturday. He stopped in the gateway of a brewery to ask the journeymen coopers where there would be dancing that evening and the next day.

There were several places, but the best was the Lion at Gertelfingen, only half an hour away. That, he decided, was where he would take Bärbele, the girl next door.

It was nearly lunchtime, and as Knulp climbed the stairs of the Rothfuss house a pleasantly pungent smell came his way. He stopped still and breathed in the balm with boyish pleasure and curiosity. Despite the lightness of his step, the tanner's wife had heard him. She flung open the kitchen door and stood in the bright opening, clouded in the steam of her cooking.

"Ah, Herr Knulp," she cried out affectionately. "I'm glad you're so early. You see, we're having liver dumplings, and I thought maybe I could fry up a slice of liver just for you, if you like. How do you feel about it?"

Knulp stroked his cheek and made a courtly gesture.

"Why should there be something special for me? I'll be only too happy with a dish of soup."

"That's no way to talk. When a man's been sick,

he needs proper nourishment, he's got to get his strength back. But maybe you don't care for liver. Some people don't."

He laughed modestly. "Oh, I'm not one of those. A dish of liver dumplings is a Sunday dinner. If I could have them every Sunday of my life, I'd be perfectly happy."

"While you're staying with us you must have everything you want. What did I learn to cook for? Just speak up. There's an extra slice of liver, I've saved it for you. It would do you good."

She came closer and gave him an encouraging smile. He understood quite well what she meant, and she *was* rather pretty, but he pretended not to notice. He played with his fine hat that the poor tailor had ironed, and looked to one side.

"Thank you, Frau Rothfuss. Thank you for your kindness. But I really prefer dumplings. You've been spoiling me enough as it is."

She smiled and threatened him with her forefinger. "You don't have to act so bashful. It doesn't convince me anyway. Dumplings then. With plenty of onions, eh?"

"I can't say no to that."

She went busily back to her stove, while he went into the big room, where the table had already been laid. He sat reading yesterday's paper until the tanner came in and the soup was served. When the meal was over, the three of them played cards for a little while, and Knulp amazed his hostess with a few hazardous and graceful new card tricks. He had a playfully negligent way of shuffling and then gathering up the deck with the speed of lightning; he tossed his card on the table with an elegant gesture and occasionally ran his thumb over the edge of his cards. The tanner watched him with the admiration and indulgence that unprofitable skills arouse in a hard-working citizen. But his wife observed these signs of *savoir-vivre* with knowing interest. Her eyes rested attentively on his long graceful hands, which no hard work had ever disfigured.

Through the small windowpanes a thin, uncertain beam of sunlight poured into the room, passed over the table and the cards, played fitfully with the faint shadows on the floor and circled tremulously round the pale-blue ceiling. Knulp's eyes sparkled as he took it all in: the play of the February sun, the peace and quiet of the house, his friend's grave, work-hardened face, and the pretty woman's veiled glances. He didn't like it, this wasn't his aim in life, this wasn't his kind of happiness. If my health were better and if it were summer, he thought, I wouldn't stay here an hour longer.

"I think I'll follow the sun for a while," he said, as Rothfuss picked up the cards and looked at the clock. He went downstairs with the tanner, left him in the drying shed with his skins, and wandered off through the dismal grass plot which extended, interspersed with tanning pits, down to the river. There the tanner had built a little board pier to stand on when washing his skins. Knulp sat down on the pier, letting his feet dangle over the swift silent stream, and watched with delight the dark fishes darting here and there below him. Then he studied his surroundings, trying to figure out a way of speaking to the little servant girl next door.

The gardens of the two houses adjoined, separated only by a broken-down lath fence. Down by the water the fence poles had long since rotted away and one could pass without difficulty from one garden to the other. The neighbor's garden seemed better-kept than the tanner's tangled grass plot. Knulp could see four little vegetable patches, overgrown with weeds as they are in the wintertime, two meager borders of lettuce and winter spinach, and a number of bowed rose bushes, their crowns buried in the ground. Farther up there were several handsome fir trees, which hid the house.

After a careful study of the neighbor's garden, Knulp crept silently as far as the fir trees; between them he could see the house, with the kitchen in back. He had not long to wait before he saw the girl, her sleeves rolled up, at work in the kitchen. The lady of the house was with her, giving orders, showing her one thing and another, as women must do when, unwilling to pay an experienced maid, they take on a beginner every year and then are always full of praises for the girl who has just left. But the tone in which she instructed and found fault was without malice; apparently the new girl was already used to it, for she went about her work calmly and with unruffled brow.

The intruder stood leaning against a tree, watching and listening with the vigilance of a hunter and the serene patience of a man whose time is cheap and who has learned to enjoy life as a spectator. It gave him pleasure to watch the young girl whenever she appeared in the window. The rest of the time he listened and gathered from her employer's speech that she was not a native of Lächstetten but of some place farther up in the valley. Chewing on a fragrant fir twig, he listened patiently for half an hour and then another half hour until at length the lady of the house disappeared and all was silent in the kitchen.

He waited a little longer, then approached quietly and tapped on the kitchen window with a dry branch. The girl paid no attention and he had to knock again. This time she came to the half-open window, opened it wide, and looked out.

"Goodness, what are you doing here?" she exclaimed in a whisper. "I almost had a fright."

"How could I frighten anybody?" said Knulp with a smile. "I just wanted to say hello and see how you were getting along. And besides, it's Saturday; I wanted to ask if you could take a little walk with me tomorrow afternoon."

She shook her head; the look on her face was so woebegone that he felt really sorry for her.

"No," she said in a friendly tone. "I won't be off tomorrow; only in the morning to go to church."

"Hm," Knulp muttered. "But then you could go out with me this evening."

"This evening? Well yes, I'll be free, but I mean to write a letter—to my people at home."

"Oh, you'll write your letter an hour later, it won't go out tonight anyway. I'd been so looking forward to a little chat with you, and we could have such a nice walk this evening, if it doesn't rain pitchforks. So be nice. You're not afraid of me, are you?"

"I'm not afraid of anybody and certainly not of you. But I can't. If they see me out walking with a man . . ."

"But Bärbele, nobody knows you here. Besides, it's no sin and it's nobody's business. You're not a schoolgirl any more. So don't forget, I'll be waiting at eight o'clock down by the gymnasium—you know, next to the cattle market. Or should I come earlier? I can if you like."

"No, not earlier. No . . . don't come at all, it's impossible, I can't . . ."

He displayed his boyish, crestfallen look.

"Well, if you don't feel like it!" he said sadly. "It seemed to me you were all alone and a stranger here and you must be homesick sometimes, and me too, and we could have talked a little. I'd have liked to hear more about Achthausen, because of being there once. But I can't force you, and don't take it amiss."

"Why would I take it amiss? It's just that I can't."

"You're free this evening, Bärbele. You just don't want to come. But maybe you'll change your mind. I've got to go now, but I'll be outside the gymnasium this evening, and if nobody comes I'll go for a walk by myself and think of you writing your letter to Achthausen. So goodbye and no hard feelings."

He gave a quick nod and was gone before she could say anything more. She saw him vanish behind the trees and a look of perplexity came over her face. Then she went back to her work and suddenly she began—the lady of the house had gone out—to sing for all she was worth.

Knulp heard her. He was sitting on the tanner's pier again, rolling little balls from a piece of bread he had put in his pocket at lunch. He dropped the bread balls gently into the water one after another, and watched musingly as they drifted a little way with the current and sank to the dark bottom, where they were snapped up by the silent ghostlike fishes.

"Well," said the tanner at supper, "here it is Saturday. You wouldn't know how good it feels after a hard week."

"Oh, I can imagine," said Knulp with a smile. Frau Rothfuss smiled, too, and gave him a mischievous look.

"Tonight," Rothfuss went on in a festive tone, "tonight we'll have a nice jug of beer together, the old lady will go and get it right away. And tomorrow, if the weather's good, the three of us will go for a hike. What do you say to that, old friend?"

Knulp gave him a good thump on the shoulder.

"It's a good life here with you, I've got to say that. I'm looking forward to our hike. But this evening I'll be busy; I have a friend here; he's been working in the upper blacksmith shop and he's leaving in the morning. —I'm sorry, but we'll have all day tomorrow together, or I wouldn't have arranged it that way."

"But you can't go running around at night when you're still half sick."

"Oh, it's no good coddling myself too much. I won't be out late. Where do you keep the key, so I can let myself in?"

"What a stubborn fellow you are! All right, go if you must. You'll find the key behind the shutters of the basement window. You know the place?"

"Of course. Well, I'll be going now. Don't stay up for me. Good night. Good night, Frau Rothfuss."

He went down the stairs and had reached the outer door when the tanner's wife came running after him. She handed him an umbrella and, like it or not, Knulp had to take it.

"You must take care of yourself, Knulp," she said. "And now I'll show you where to find the key."

She took him by the hand in the darkness, led him around in back, and stopped by a little window.

"We put the key behind the shutters," she said in an excited whisper and stroked Knulp's hand. "Just reach in through the opening, it will be on the windowsill."

"Thank you," said Knulp, and withdrew his hand in embarrassment.

"Can I save you a mug of beer?" she asked, pressing gently close to him.

"No, thanks. I don't usually drink any at night. Good night, Frau Rothfuss, and thank you."

She gave his arm a squeeze and whispered affectionately: "Are you in such a hurry?" Her face was close to his and in the awkward silence, not wishing to push her away forcibly, he ran his hand over her hair. "But now I must be going," he said in an exaggeratedly loud voice, and stepped back.

She smiled at him with parted lips, he could see her teeth shining in the darkness. And very softly she said: "Then I'll wait till you come home. You're a dear."

He walked quickly away into the dark street with his umbrella under his arm, and at the next corner, to get rid of his silly uneasiness, he began to whistle the tune of a song:

You think I'm going to take you.
Oh no, you're not for me.
Shame makes me want to shake you
When I'm in company.

The air was balmy, and here and there a star appeared in the black sky. In one of the inns some young people were having a boisterous Saturday night, and behind the windows of the new bowling alley at the Peacock he saw a group of substantial citizens in shirt-sleeves, weighing bowling balls in their hands and smoking cigars.

At the gymnasium Knulp stopped and looked around. The damp wind sang softly in the bare chestnut trees, the river flowed soundlessly in the deep darkness, broken only by the reflections of a window or two. The gentle night soothed the tramp in every fiber of his being, he sniffed the air with an intimation of spring, warm weather, and dry roads. His inexhaustible memory surveyed the city, the river valley, and the whole region; he knew it well, he knew the roads and the paths along the river, the villages, hamlets, and farms, and he knew where he could expect a friendly lodging for the night. He thought hard, planning his next journey since he could stay in Lächstetten no longer. But he wanted to stay over Sunday for his friend's sake, if the woman didn't make it too hard for him.

Perhaps, he reflected, he ought to have said something to the tanner about his wife. But he didn't like to meddle in other people's concerns, and he felt no need to try to make people better or wiser. He was sorry it had turned out this way, and his feelings toward the former waitress at the Ox were not at all friendly; but at the same time he had to laugh when he thought of the tanner's pompous speeches about the joys of domesticity and marriage. He knew about these things. When a man boasted of his happiness or his virtue, they usually didn't amount to much; the same had been true of the tailor's piety. You could observe people's folly, you could laugh at them or feel sorry for them, but you had to let them go their own way.

With a deep sigh he dismissed these matters and, propping himself against the bend of an old chestnut tree across from the bridge, turned his thoughts back to his travels. He would have liked to tramp through the Black Forest, but it was too cold in the mountains at this season, most likely the ground was still covered with snow; you ruined your boots, and places to spend the night were too far apart. No, that wouldn't do. He would have to follow the valleys and stick to the towns. Stag's Mill, four hours down the river, was the first reliable stopping place; they would surely keep him for two days if the weather was bad.

Deep in his thoughts, he had just about forgotten that he was waiting for someone when a frail frightened figure appeared on the dark wind-swept bridge and came hesitantly closer. He recognized her at once; happy and grateful, he ran to meet her, swinging his hat.

"Bärbele! How nice of you to come! I'd almost stopped expecting you."

Walking at her left side, he led her up the river walk. She was timid and shy.

"I really shouldn't have come," she said over and over again. "If only nobody sees us!"

But Knulp had all sorts of questions to ask and soon her step became calmer and steadier. In a little while she was chatting with him as easily as an old friend. Encouraged by his questions and comments, she told him about her village, her father and mother, her brother and grandma, about the ducks and chickens, the hailstorms and sicknesses, the weddings and fairs. Her little treasure of experiences opened up, and it was larger than she herself would have supposed. At length she told him how her parents had hired her out and she had left home, and went on to speak of her work and the household she was in.

They were far out of town before Bärbele gave a

thought to where they were going. Her chatter had set her free from a long dreary week of loneliness, of doing as she was told and saying nothing. She was all cheered up.

"But where are we?" she suddenly cried in amazement. "Where are we going?"

"If it's all right with you, we're going to Gertelfingen, we're nearly there."

"Gertelfingen? What for? We'd better go back, it's getting late."

"When do you have to be back, Bärbele?"

"At ten. Very soon. It's been a nice walk."

"Ten o'clock is a long way off," said Knulp. "I'll see that you get home on time. But we'll never again be so young together, so I thought we might risk a dance. Or don't you like to dance?"

She looked at him with eager surprise. "I love to dance. But where? Out here in the night?"

"We'll be in Gertelfingen in a minute and there's music at the Lion. We could go in for just one dance, and then we'll go home and we'll have had a fine evening."

Bärbele stopped still, thinking it over.

"It would be fun," she said slowly. "But what will people think of us? I don't want to be taken for that kind of girl, and I wouldn't want anybody to think we're going together either."

Suddenly she laughed gaily and said: "You see, if I

have a sweetheart later on, it mustn't be a tanner. I don't want to offend you, but tanning is a dirty trade."

"Maybe you've got something there," said Knulp good-naturedly. "I don't expect you to marry me. But nobody here knows I'm a tanner or that you're so proud, and I've washed my hands, so if you'd care to dance once around with me, you're invited. If not, we'll turn back."

A pale gable belonging to the first house of the village peered out through the black foliage. Suddenly Knulp said "Pst!" and lifted a finger: the sound of dance music from the village, an accordion and a fiddle.

"All right!" Bärbele laughed and they walked faster.

At the Lion only four or five couples were dancing, all young people unknown to Knulp. The atmosphere was quiet and sedate and no one molested the strangers who joined in the next dance. They danced a ländler and a polka and then came a waltz. Bärbele didn't know how to waltz, so they sat down and had a drop of beer, which was as far as Knulp's finances went.

Bärbele was flushed from dancing, and her eyes sparkled as she looked on.

"I suppose it's time to go," said Knulp at half past nine.

She started in surprise and looked rather sad.

"What a shame!" she said softly.

"We could stay a little longer."

"No. I've got to get back. It's been lovely."

They left the room but at the door something occurred to Bärbele: "We haven't given the musicians anything."

"No," said Knulp with some embarrassment. "They deserve a tenner. The trouble is, I haven't got one."

Eagerly she drew her little knitted purse from her pocket. "Why didn't you say anything? Here. Give it to them."

He took the coin and gave it to the musicians, then they left. Outside, they had to wait a few minutes before they could see the way in the deep darkness. The wind was blowing harder, driving an occasional raindrop before it.

"Should I put up the umbrella?" Knulp asked.

"No, we'd never get ahead in this wind. It was nice in there. You dance almost like a dancing master, tanner."

She went on chattering gaily. Her friend had fallen silent, perhaps because he was tired, perhaps because he dreaded the impending leave-taking.

All at once she began to sing: "I graze by the Neckar, I graze by the Rhine." Her voice was warm and pure. At the second verse Knulp joined in and sang the bass part with such sureness and in such a fine deep voice that she listened happily.

"Well," he asked at the end, "is your homesickness gone?"

"Oh yes," she said, laughing brightly. "We must take another walk soon."

"I'm sorry," he said more softly. "I'm afraid this is the last."

She stopped still. She hadn't quite heard the words, but she had caught the note of dejection.

"But what's wrong?" she asked tremulously. "Are you put out with me?"

"Of course not, Bärbele. But I've got to be leaving tomorrow. I've given notice."

"You don't mean it. Really? Oh, I am sorry to hear that."

"You mustn't be sorry about me. I wouldn't have stayed very long in any case, and besides I'm only a tanner. You must find a sweetheart soon, a handsome young fellow. Then you'll never be homesick again. You'll see."

"Don't talk like that. You know I like you very much, even if you're not my sweetheart."

They were both silent. The wind whistled round their faces. Knulp walked more slowly. They were almost at the bridge. At length he stopped still.

"I'll bid you goodbye now. You'd better go the rest of the way by yourself."

With sincere affliction Bärbele looked into his face.

"So it's true? Then let me thank you. I'll never forget this evening. And good luck."

He clasped her hand and drew her close to him. Frightened and surprised, she looked into his eyes. Then he took her head with its rain-wet braids in both hands and whispered: "Goodbye, Bärbele. But before I go, I want a kiss from you, so you won't forget me entirely."

She trembled and shrank back a little, but his eyes were kindly and sad, and now for the first time she noticed how fine they were. Gravely, without closing her own, she accepted his kiss. Then when he stood hesitant, a faint smile on his lips, tears welled to her eyes and she returned his kiss with warmth.

She walked away quickly and was already on the bridge when suddenly she turned round and came back. He was still standing on the same spot.

"What is it, Bärbele?" he asked. "You must go home."

"Oh yes, I'm going. You mustn't think badly of me."

"Certainly not."

"But tell me, tanner. You said you had no money. Won't you be paid before you go?"

"No, there's no pay coming to me. But that's nothing. I'll manage. You mustn't worry."

"No, no! You've got to have something in your pocket. Here!"

She pressed a large coin into his hand; he knew by the feel that it was a taler.

"You can give it back to me or send it sometime."

He held her hand.

"It won't do. You mustn't throw your money around like this. Why, it's a whole taler. Take it back. I insist. If you have some small change, say fifty pfennigs, I'll take it gladly because I'm hard up. But no more."

They argued a little longer, and Bärbele had to show him her purse, because she said she had nothing but the taler. But this wasn't true, she also had a mark and one of the little silver twenty-pfennig pieces that were still current. He wanted to take that, but she said it wasn't enough; then he said he wouldn't take anything, but finally he kept the mark piece, and she rushed off.

On the way home she wondered why he hadn't kissed her again, now with a sense of regret, now with the feeling that in not kissing her again he had been really sweet and considerate. And this was the feeling she ended up with.

It was more than an hour later when Knulp came home. He saw that the light was still on in the big room, which meant that the tanner's wife was sitting up waiting for him. He spat with annoyance and thought of running off into the night that very minute. But he was tired, it was going to rain, and he didn't want to be unkind to the tanner. And besides he felt like playing a harmless little joke.

He fished the key out of its hiding place, opened the house door as stealthily as a thief, closed it behind him, locked it soundlessly with tight-pressed lips, and carefully put the key in its place. Then he took off his shoes and climbed the stairs in his stocking feet. The door to the big room was ajar. He saw light through the crack and heard the tanner's wife, who had fallen asleep from the long wait, breathing deeply on the sofa. Then he climbed silently to his room, locked himself in, and went to bed. But the next day—his mind was made up—he would leave.

MY RECOLLECTIONS OF KNULP

My Recollections of Knulp

IN THOSE DAYS I was young and gay, and Knulp was still alive. It was midsummer; the two of us were tramping through fertile country and had few worries. By day we sauntered through yellow grain-fields or lay in the cool shade of a walnut tree or at the edge of the forest, and at night I listened and looked on as Knulp told the peasants stories, put on shadow plays for the children, or sang his songs for the girls. I listened with pleasure and without envy; only when he was standing surrounded by girls, his tanned face flashing like summer lightning, when for all their laughing and joking the young things couldn't take their eyes off him, it occasionally struck me that he was an uncommonly lucky devil or that I myself was the opposite. And then, sick of sitting there like a bump on a log, I sometimes crept away by myself and dropped in on the village priest for a sensible talk and a night's lodging, or went to the tavern for a quiet glass of wine.

One afternoon, I remember, as we were making our way through the fields, far from the nearest village, we came to a deserted graveyard with a little chapel beside it. Surrounded by walls overgrown with dark shrubbery, it lay friendly and peaceful in the hot countryside. There were two large chestnut trees at the entrance. The gate was closed and I wanted to go on. Not so Knulp, who started climbing over the wall.

"Stopping again?" I asked.

"I think so. I wouldn't want to get sore feet."

"But does it have to be a graveyard?"

"Never mind. Just come along. I know that peasants don't go in much for pleasure, but when it comes to their last resting place, they like their comfort. It's worth a bit of trouble to them, they grow the loveliest things on their graves and all around them."

I joined him in climbing the low wall and saw that he was right. The graves, most of them marked by white wooden crosses, lay in straight and crooked rows, and over them grew flowers and greenery. Bindweed and geraniums sparkled with joy, late gillyflowers grew in the shadier spots, there were rose bushes weighed down with roses, and a dense copse of lilac and elder.

We looked about for a while and then sat down in the grass, which in places was tall and in flower. We rested and cooled off and a feeling of contentment came over us.

Knulp read the name on the nearest cross and said: "His name was Engelbert Auer, he lived to be over sixty. But now he's lying under mignonette, which is a lovely flower, and he's at peace. I'd be glad to have some mignonette myself when the time comes; in the meantime, I'll take a little of this."

I said: "Better take something else; mignonette fades so soon."

However, he broke off a sprig and put it in his hat, which was lying beside him on the grass.

"How wonderfully quiet it is!" I said.

And he: "Yes, indeed. If it were just a little quieter, we could hear them talking down there."

"Not them. They've finished talking."

"How do we know? They say that death is sleep; don't we talk in our sleep now and then? Sometimes we even sing."

"Maybe you do."

"Why not? If I were dead, I'd wait until Sunday when the girls come out here to look about and pick flowers from the graves, and then I'd start singing, but very softly."

"What would you sing?"

"What I'd sing? Oh, any old song."

He stretched out on the ground, closed his eyes, and soon began to sing in a soft, childlike voice:

Because I've died so young,
Come sing me, pretty maidens,
A song of farewell.

When I come back again,
When I come back again,
I'll be a pretty lad.

I couldn't help laughing, though I liked the song. He sang beautifully, and even if the words didn't always make sense, the tune was lovely and that was enough.

"Knulp," I said, "don't promise the pretty maidens too much, or they'll stop listening to you. It's all very well to say you'll come back, but no one really knows about these things, and how can you be sure you'll be a pretty lad?"

"No, I can't be sure; that's a fact. But that's what I'd like to be. Remember the other day, the little boy with the cow that we asked the way of? I wish I could be like him when I come back. Don't you?"

"No, not I. I once knew an old man, well over seventy, his eyes were so quiet and kindly; it seemed to me that everything about him was kindly and wise and quiet. Ever since then, I've thought that if I came back I'd want to be like him."

"Well, you've got a long way to go. Altogether it's a funny thing about wishes. If all I had to do this minute was to nod and I'd be a nice little boy like that, and all you had to do was nod and you'd be a kindly old man, neither of us would nod. We'd be quite pleased to stay just as we are."

"Yes, that's true."

"It's true, all right. But that's not all. Sometimes I say to myself that the most beautiful thing in the world is a slender young girl with blond hair. But that's nonsense, because often enough we see a brunette who seems to be almost more beautiful. And besides, there are other times when I think the most beautiful thing of all is a bird soaring free in the sky. And another time nothing seems so marvelous as a butterfly, a white one for instance with red dots on its wings, or the sun shining in the clouds at evening, when the whole world is aglow, yet the light doesn't dazzle us, and everything looks so happy and innocent."

"Right you are, Knulp. Everything is beautiful when you look at it in a good moment."

"Yes. But there's more to it. The most beautiful things, I think, give us something else beside pleasure; they also leave us with a feeling of sadness or fear."

"Why?"

"I mean that a beautiful girl wouldn't seem so beautiful if we didn't know that she has her season and that when it's over she'll grow old and die. If a beautiful thing were to remain beautiful for all eternity, I'd be glad, but all the same I'd look at it with a colder eye. I'd say to myself: You can look at it any time, it doesn't have to be today. But when I know that something is perishable and can't last forever, I look at it with a feeling not just of joy but of compassion as well."

"I suppose so."

"To me there's nothing more beautiful than fireworks in the night. There are blue and green fireballs, they rise up in the darkness, and at the height of their beauty they double back and they're gone. When you watch them, you're happy but at the same time afraid, because in a moment it will all be over. The happiness and the fear go together, and it's much more beautiful than if it lasted longer. Don't you feel the same way?"

"Yes, I think I do. But that's not true of everything."

"Why not?"

"For instance, if a boy and girl love each other and get married, or if two people get to be friends, it's beautiful because it's meant to last and not to end right away."

Knulp looked at me closely; then his black lashes flickered and he said thoughtfully: "Yes. But that comes to an end too, like everything else. All sorts of things can wreck a friendship, or a love for that matter."

"True, but we don't think of that until it happens."

"I don't know about that. —For instance, I've had two loves in my life, real ones I mean, and each time I knew it would last forever and could end only with death, but each time it ended, and I didn't die. I had a friend too, back home, and I thought we'd never part. But we did part, long long ago."

He fell silent and I could think of nothing to say. I still had no experience of the sorrow that is part and parcel of every human relationship, nor had I learned that no matter how close two human beings may be, there is always a gulf between them which only love can bridge, and that only from hour to hour. I pondered my friend's words; I liked best what he had said about the fireballs, because I myself had often had the same feeling. The quiet spell of the colored flame, rising into the darkness and all too soon drowning in it, struck me as a symbol of all human pleasure, for the more beautiful it is, the less it satisfies us and the more quickly it is spent. I told Knulp what I had been thinking.

But he wouldn't go into it. He only said "Yes . . . yes." And then, after a long while, in a muffled voice: "There's no sense in all this brooding and pondering; we never do what we think. We don't stop to reflect, we do what our hearts bid us. But maybe there's something in what I said about friendship and love. In the end, we all have a life of our own that we can't share with anyone else. You can see that when a friend or loved one dies. You weep and grieve for a day, a month, or even a year, but then the dear departed is dead and gone, and the person in the coffin might just as well be some homeless unknown apprentice."

"Don't say that, Knulp, I don't like it. We've often talked about these things. We've always said that life must have a meaning and that there is a point in being good and friendly rather than bad and unfriendly. But the way you're talking now, nothing makes any difference and we could just as well be thieves and murderers."

"No, my friend, we couldn't. See if you can bring yourself to murder the next few people we meet. Or tell a yellow butterfly that it ought to be blue. It will laugh in your face."

"That's not what I mean. But if nothing matters, then there's no point in trying to be good and upright. There's no goodness if blue is as good as yellow and evil is as good as good. Then a man is the same as an animal in the woods; he simply follows his nature and there's neither virtue nor guilt."

Knulp sighed.

"What can I say? Maybe you're right. And that's why we get these stupid fits of gloom, because we feel that our wanting and trying are meaningless and that things simply go their own way. But there's guilt even so, even when a man can't help being bad. Because he's aware of the badness in him. And that's why goodness must be the right way, because when we do good we're happy and our conscience is clear."

I could see by his face that he was sick of this discussion. That often happened with him. He started philosophizing, stated principles, argued for and against, and then suddenly stopped. At first I thought he had had enough of my inept answers and objections. But it wasn't that; he felt that his leaning to speculation carried him into territory where his knowledge and means of expression were inadequate. For though he had read a great deal, Tolstoy for instance, he was not always able to distinguish between sound and unsound reasoning, and he himself sensed as much. He spoke of learned men as a gifted child speaks of adults; he had to admit that they were stronger and better equipped than he, but he despised them for making no proper use of their learning and for solving no riddles with all their wisdom.

Now he was lying on his back again with his head cradled in his hands, peering through the black elder leaves into the hot blue sky and softly singing an old Rhenish folk song. I still recall the last stanza:

I've worn the red coat until now,
And now the black coat I must wear
Seven years to the day,
Till my love rots away.

Late in the afternoon we sat facing each other at the dark edge of a copse, each with a big chunk of bread and half a hard sausage, eating and watching the night fall. Only a short time before, the hills had been bright with the yellow glow of the evening sky, bathed in a fluffy luminous haze; now they were dark and sharply outlined, painting their trees, bushes, and meadows on the sky, which still had a little light blue in it but much more of the dark blue of the night.

While there was light enough, we had read nonsense to each other out of *Strains from the German Hurdy-gurdy*, a little book of idiotic songs illustrated with small woodcuts. That had ended with the daylight. When we had done eating, Knulp wanted music. I pulled my harmonica from my pocket, which was full of crumbs, wiped it, and played our usual half-dozen tunes. The darkness had spread far over the rolling countryside, the sky had lost its pale glow and in growing darker had shot forth one star after another. The light, thin notes of the harmonica flew over the fields and lost themselves in the distance.

"It's too early to sleep," I said to Knulp. "Tell me a story—it doesn't have to be true—or a fairy tale."

Knulp thought back.

"All right," he said. "A story and a fairy tale, both in one. You see, it's a dream. I had this dream last fall and twice more since then, almost the same. Here it is:

"A narrow street in a small town like the one I come from. All the houses had gables overlooking the street, but they were higher than the ones you usually see.

I was walking through the street. It was as though I were coming home after a long long time, but I wasn't really happy, because something was wrong. I had a feeling that maybe I was in the wrong place, that this wasn't my home town at all. Some parts of it were exactly as they should have been and I recognized them at once, but many houses were strange and deserted, and I couldn't find the bridge that led to the marketplace; instead, I passed an unfamiliar garden and a church that was like in Cologne or Basel, with two big steeples. Our church at home had no steeple at all, but only a low stump with a make-shift roof, because the builders had made a mistake and hadn't been able to finish the steeple.

"It was the same with the people. I recognized some that I saw in the distance, I knew their names, I had them on my lips and I was all ready to call out. But most of them went into houses or side streets and were gone. When one of them came closer, he turned into a stranger; then when he had passed me and I looked after him, it seemed to me that he was the man after all and that I did know him. I saw a group of women standing outside a shop, and one of them, I thought, was my aunt, who is dead; but when I went up to them, I no longer recognized her, and they were speaking a strange dialect that I could hardly understand.

"In the end I thought: Oh, if I could only be gone

from here, it's my old town and then again it isn't. But all the while I kept seeing a familiar house or a familiar face and rushing up to it, and every time I was disappointed. But I wasn't angry or vexed, only sad and afraid; I wanted to say a prayer and tried hard to remember one, but all I could think of was silly phrases—such as 'Dear Sir' and 'Under the circumstances'—and in my sadness and confusion I went about mumbling these.

"This, it seemed to me, lasted a few hours, until I was thoroughly hot and tired, and still I stumbled aimlessly from place to place. By then it was evening and I decided to ask the next person I met where I could lodge for the night or how to find the road out of town, but I was unable to speak to anyone, they all passed me by as though I weren't there. I was so tired and desperate I thought I'd burst into tears.

"Then suddenly I turned a corner and there was our old street. It had changed, it looked unreal and ornate, but by then that didn't trouble me much. I walked along and distinctly recognized house after house in spite of the dream decorations, and finally I came to the old house where I grew up. Like the others, it was unnaturally tall, but otherwise it looked pretty much as it had in the old days, and I shuddered with joy and excitement.

"In the doorway stood my first love, her name was Henriette. Except that she was taller and somehow different than before, and still more beautiful. As I came closer, I saw that there was something miraculous and angelic about her beauty, but I also noticed that her hair was golden blond and not brown like Henriette's; still, it was Henriette from top to toe, though transfigured.

" 'Henriette!' I cried out, and took off my hat because she looked so ethereal that I wasn't sure she'd recognize me.

"She turned and looked into my eyes. And as she looked into my eyes, I was surprised and ashamed, because it wasn't Henriette but Lisabeth, my second love, whom I had gone with for years.

"So I cried 'Lisabeth!' and held out my hand.

"She looked at me; her look pierced my heart, as if God had looked at me; it wasn't severe or proud but clear and calm, yet so spiritual and lofty that I felt like a dog. And as she looked at me, she became grave and sad; then she shook her head as if I had asked an impudent question. She didn't take my hand but went back into the house and closed the door behind her. I could hear the lock snap.

"I turned around and went away, and though I was almost blinded by tears and grief, I saw that the city was strangely changed. For now every street and every house was exactly as it had been in the old days, the evil spell was broken. The gables were no longer so high and the colors were right, the people were really themselves and looked at me with happy surprise as though they knew me, and some called me by name. But I couldn't answer and I couldn't stop to talk with them. Something drove me across the old familiar bridge and out of the city, and my heart was so sore that tears clouded everything I saw. I didn't know why, but it seemed to me that I had lost everything I had in the city and was running away in disgrace.

"Under the poplars at the edge of the town I stopped to rest. Only then did it occur to me that I had been right outside our old home and hadn't given a thought to my father and mother, my brothers, sisters, and friends. Never had my heart been filled with such turmoil, grief, and shame. But I couldn't turn back and make amends, because the dream was over and I woke up."

Knulp said: "Every human being has his soul, he can't mix it with any other. Two people can meet, they can talk with one another, they can be close together. But their souls are like flowers, each rooted to its place. One can't go to another, because it would have to break away from its roots, and that it can't do. Flowers send out their scent and their seeds, because they would like to go to each other; but a flower can't do anything to make a seed go to its right place; the wind does that, and the wind comes and goes where it pleases."

And later: "Maybe that's what the dream I told you means. I didn't wrong Henriette or Lisabeth knowingly. But because I once loved them both and wanted to make them my own, they became for me a kind of dream figure, which looks like both of them and is neither. That figure belongs to me, but it no longer has life. And I've often had such thoughts about my parents. They think I'm their child and that I'm like them. But though I love them, I'm a stranger to them, a stranger they can't understand. And to them the main part of me, what may actually be my soul, is unimportant; they put it down to my youth, or to caprice. And yet they love me and would do anything in the world for me. A father can pass on his nose and eyes and even his intelligence to his child, but not his soul. In every human being the soul is new."

I had nothing to say to that, for at the time I hadn't begun to think along those lines, at least I had felt no inner need to. Such musings didn't dismay me in the least; they didn't touch my heart and so I imagined that for Knulp as well they were more a game than a struggle. Besides, it was so lovely and peaceful to be lying side by side in the dry grass, waiting for night and sleep and watching the first stars.

I said: "You're a thinker, Knulp. You ought to have been a professor."

He laughed and shook his head. "I'd be much more

likely to join the Salvation Army one of these days," he said thoughtfully.

That was too much. "I don't believe you," I said. "Next you'll be telling me you want to become a saint."

"So I do, so I do. Everybody who's really in earnest about what he thinks and does is a saint. If he thinks something is right, he's got to do it. And if one day I think it's right for me to join the Salvation Army, I hope I'll do it."

"Why the Salvation Army?"

"I'll tell you why. I've spoken with a lot of people and listened to a lot of speeches. I've listened to priests and schoolteachers and mayors and Social Democrats and Liberals; but deep in his heart not a one of them was in earnest; not a one made me feel that if need be he'd sacrifice himself for his wisdom. But in the Salvation Army, with all the music and ruckus, I've seen and heard two or three fellows who were really in earnest."

"How do you know?"

"Never mind, you can tell. I remember one who was making a speech in a village square one Sunday. With the heat and the dust, his voice left him. He didn't look very strong. When he couldn't get out another word, he let his three companions sing a verse of a hymn, and he drank a little water. Half the village were standing around him, children and grownups, they made fun of him and heckled him. Behind him there was a young farm hand with a whip. From time to time he snapped it, crack!—to plague the speaker, and everybody laughed. But the poor fellow didn't get angry, though he wasn't stupid; he struggled against the hubbub with his poor weak voice and smiled where anyone else would have wept or cursed. You know, a man doesn't do that for starvation wages or for pleasure; no, there's got to be a great clarity and certainty inside him."

"Possibly. But the same thing won't do for everybody. A clever, sensitive man like you couldn't stand all that noise."

"Maybe he could. If he had something and knew something that was better than all his cleverness and sensitiveness. I know the same thing won't do for everybody, but the truth has to do."

"Oh, the truth! How do we know that those halleluiah singers have the truth?"

"You've got something there. We don't know. I'm only saying that if one day I find it's the truth, I'll follow it."

"If! But every day you find some piece of wisdom, and the next day you give it up."

He looked at me in consternation. "That wasn't a nice thing to say."

I wanted to apologize, but he stopped me and fell silent. In a little while he softly said good night and stretched out, but I don't think he fell asleep right away. I was wide awake myself and lay there for over an hour propped up on my elbows, peering into the night.

In the morning I saw right away that this was one of Knulp's good days. I told him so. He beamed at me out of his childlike eyes and said: "You've guessed right. And do you know where a good day like this comes from?"

"No. Where?"

"From sleeping well and dreaming of beautiful things. But you mustn't remember what they were. That's how it is with me today. I've dreamed magnificent, joyful things, but I've forgotten them all; I only know it was wonderful."

Even before we came to the next village and had our morning milk under our belts, he sang four brand-new songs into the sober morning in his warm, light, effortless voice. Written out and printed, these songs might not amount to much. Knulp was not a great poet, but a poet he was, and while he was singing them, his little songs often bore a close family resemblance to the finest songs in the world. Certain passages and lines that I remember are really beautiful and I still cherish them. They were never written down; his verses were born, lived, and died like the breezes, in irresponsible innocence, but they gave beauty and warmth to many a moment, not only for himself and me but for many others as well.

That morning he sang the praises of the sun, as he did in nearly all his songs.

Like a maiden from her door,
Bright and clad in Sunday best,
Blushing and yet proudly, she
Steps up from the mountain crest.

His conversation was often heavy with philosophy, but his songs had the lightness of children playing in their summer clothes. Some of them were nothing but whimsical nonsense, a mere outlet for his high spirits.

That day I was infected by his mood. We called out greetings to all the people we met and teased them, sometimes leaving laughter behind us and sometimes abuse, and our whole day passed like a holiday. We told each other jokes from our schooldays and recalled schoolboy pranks, we made up nicknames for the peasants who passed and sometimes for their horses and oxen, we stopped by a garden fence that could not be seen from the road and stuffed ourselves full of gooseberries, and we economized on energy and shoe leather by taking a rest every hour or so.

It seemed to me that never in the course of our brief friendship had I seen Knulp so merry and bright and entertaining. This, I thought to my delight, was the true beginning of our happy vagrant life together.

By midday the heat grew oppressive and we spent more time lying in the grass than walking. Late in the afternoon, storm clouds gathered, the air was still and sultry, and we decided to seek shelter for the night.

Knulp became less talkative; he was a little tired, but I hardly noticed it, for he continued to laugh heartily when I laughed and to sing when I sang. I myself became more exuberant than ever, as though fireworks were flaring up inside me. It may have been the exact opposite with Knulp; perhaps his holiday lights had begun to die down. I was always like that at the time. On a good day, I grew more and more lively toward nightfall; if I had been enjoying myself, I couldn't stop; many a time I roamed about for hours all by myself, long after the others had gone wearily to sleep.

My afternoon exuberance took hold of me that day. Descending the valley, we came to a good-sized village and I looked forward to a riotous night. First we selected our night lodging, an easily accessible barn off to one side, then we went into the village and sat down in the garden of an inn, for I had asked my friend to be my guest that evening. Since it was a day of rejoicing, I thought we'd have pancakes and a few bottles of beer.

Knulp had accepted the invitation gladly. But when we were seated at a table under a magnificent plane tree, he said with some embarrassment: "No drinking bout, eh? I'll be glad to drink a bottle of beer, it will do me good and I'll enjoy it, but that's about all I can take."

I didn't argue. I thought: We'll have as much or as little as we please. We ate the hot pancakes with good fresh rye bread. I have to admit I ordered a second bottle of beer while Knulp's first bottle was still half full. I was overjoyed to be at such a nice inn again, sitting so grandly and comfortably, and I was in no hurry to leave.

When Knulp had finished his bottle of beer, I offered him another but he declined; instead, he suggested that we take a little walk around the village and go to bed early. This wasn't at all what I had in mind. I couldn't tell him so directly, but since my bottle wasn't empty yet, I raised no objection to his leaving ahead of me; we'd find each other later on.

And leave he did. I watched him as he descended the two or three steps and with his easy, carefree holiday gait made his way down the broad street leading to the center of the village. He had a starflower behind his ear. I was sorry he hadn't wanted to join me in another bottle of beer, but as I looked after him I thought affectionately: What a fine fellow!

Meanwhile, the sun had disappeared, the heat became more oppressive. In such weather I enjoyed sitting quietly over a cool drink. I settled myself comfortably at my table and prepared to stay awhile. Since I was just about the only guest, the waitress had plenty of time to chat with me. I ordered two cigars. One of them was originally intended for Knulp, but after a while I forgot that and smoked it myself.

About an hour later Knulp came back and tried to take me away. But I had grown roots. He said he was tired, and we agreed that he should go to our sleeping place and lie down. And he left me. No sooner had he gone than the waitress began to question me about him; the girls always took a shine to him. I didn't mind, he was my friend and she wasn't my sweetheart. I sang his praises, for I was feeling fine and I loved the whole world.

It was beginning to thunder and the wind was whistling softly in the plane tree when finally, very late, I prepared to leave. I paid, gave the girl a tenner, and started off without haste. I had gone some time without drinking, and now I felt that I'd had a bottle too many. But I could hold my drink and my bit of tipsiness only made me gay. I sang as I went, and after a while I found our sleeping quarters. I went in quietly. As I expected, I found Knulp asleep. He had spread out his brown jacket and lay on it in his shirtsleeves. His forehead, his bare neck, and one outstretched hand shone pale in the half darkness.

Then I lay down fully dressed, but my excitement and the merry-go-round in my head kept waking me, and there was light in the sky when I finally fell into a deep dull sleep—deep but not peaceful. I felt heavy and sluggish and had muddled, tormenting dreams.

I awoke late; it was already broad daylight and the brightness hurt my eyes. My head was empty and be-clouded and my bones ached. I yawned and yawned, rubbed my eyes, and stretched so hard that my joints cracked. But for all my weariness I still retained a vestige and echo of yesterday's bright humor and I felt sure I could wash away my aches and pains at the nearest well.

I was wrong. When I looked around, Knulp wasn't there. I called out to him and whistled, suspecting nothing at first. But when my calling, whistling, and searching proved vain, it suddenly came to me that he had left me. Yes, he was gone, he had crept away without a word, he hadn't wanted to stay with me any longer. Maybe my drinking had disgusted him, maybe he had been ashamed of his own exuberance the day before. Or possibly a sudden whim had come over him, or he was tired of my company, or he simply felt the need to be alone. But more than likely, my drinking had been to blame.

The joy went out of me, I was overcome with shame and grief. Where was my friend now? In spite of his speeches, I had prided myself on understanding his soul a little and on holding some share in it. And now he was gone, I was disappointed and alone. I found more fault with myself than with him. Now it was my turn to taste the loneliness which in Knulp's opinion was the lot of every man and which I had never really believed in. It was bitter, and not only on that first day. Since then, of course, it has been alleviated now and then, but it has never left me entirely.

THE END

The End

It was a bright day in October. Short, fitful gusts of wind stirred the light, sun-warmed air. The pale-blue smoke of brush fires rose in thin hesitant ribbons from fields and gardens, filling the luminous countryside with the sweet pungent smell of burning green wood and weeds. The village gardens were abloom with full-colored asters, pale late roses and dahlias; here and there along the fences a flaming nasturtium still glowed amid the pale withered shrubbery.

Dr. Machold's fly drove slowly along the gently rising road to Bulach. The grainfields on the left had already been mowed, but the potatoes were still being harvested; on the right there was a narrow strip of young pines, a brown wall of serried trunks and withered branches; the ground was of the same dry brown color, carpeted with parched pine needles. The road led straight into the tender-blue autumn sky, as though the world ended at the top of the rise.

The doctor held the reins loosely, letting his old nag go where he pleased. He had just left the deathbed of a woman who, though beyond help, had struggled obstinately for her life to the last. Now he was tired and the quiet ride through the friendly country lulled him. His thoughts had fallen asleep; absently following the cries that mingled with the smell of the brush fires, he was led to pleasant blurred memories of autumn holidays from school, and further back to the sounds and shapeless half-light of infancy. For he had grown up in the country, and his senses responded knowingly and gladly to the signs of the season and its occupations.

He had almost fallen asleep when his carriage stopped, jolting him awake. A rivulet running across the road held the front wheels in place; gratefully the horse had stopped and was waiting with lowered head, enjoying the rest.

Aroused by the sudden silence, Machold took a firm hold on the reins, smiled to see the woods and the sky sunny and clear after his few minutes of twilight, and with a friendly click of his tongue started the horse off again. Then he pulled himself up straight—he didn't approve of dozing in the daytime—and lit a cigar. The nag went on at a slow walk; two women in broad-brimmed hats called greetings from behind a long row of filled potato sacks.

By now the top of the slope was near; the horse raised his head in expectation, looking forward to the long downhill trot home. Just then a man appeared on the bright nearby horizon, a wayfarer. For a moment he stood tall and free against the glittering blue; then, descending the slope, he became gray and small. He came closer, a thin man with a small beard, poorly dressed, obviously at home on the road. His gait was weary and painful, but he lifted his hat graciously and said *Grüss Gott.*

"Grüss Gott," said Dr. Machold, and looked after the stranger when he had passed. Then suddenly he stopped his horse. Rising to his feet and turning back over the creaking carriage top, he called out: "Hey! Come here a minute!"

The dusty wayfarer stopped and looked back. He smiled faintly, turned away and seemed about to go on, then he changed his mind and complied.

Now he was standing hat in hand beside the fly.

"May I ask where you're going?" said Machold.

"Straight ahead—to Berchtoldsegg."

"Don't we know each other? It's only the name that escapes me. You know me, don't you?"

"I'd say you were Dr. Machold."

"What did I tell you? But what's your name?"

"You must know me, doctor. We were in Plocher's class together; you used to copy my Latin exercises."

Machold jumped out and looked the man in the eye. Then he laughed and slapped him on the back.

"That's it!" he said. "You're the famous Knulp, and we were classmates. Let me shake your hand, old friend! It must be ten years since we last met. Still on the road?"

"Still on the road. A man gets set in his ways as he gets older."

"That's true. But where are you heading? Back home again?"

"That's right. I'm going to Gerbersau, I've a little something to attend to."

"I see. Any of your people still living?"

"No, there's nobody left."

"You don't look exactly young any more, Knulp. We're only in our forties, you and I. And you wanting to pass me by like that, that wasn't nice of you. —You know, I think you might need a doctor."

"There's nothing much wrong with me, and what there is, no doctor can cure."

"We'll see about that. Just hop in and come along. We can talk better that way."

Knulp stepped back a little and put his hat on. With a look of embarrassment, he resisted when the doctor tried to help him into the carriage.

"What for?" he said. "Your horse won't run away while we're standing here."

But then a fit of coughing came over him and the doctor, who by then knew what was what, grabbed hold of him without further ado and boosted him into the fly.

"There," he said, driving on. "We'll be at the top in a minute. From then on it's a trot and we'll be home in half an hour. You don't have to say anything now with your cough, we can talk when we get home. —What? —No, none of that! The place for sick people is bed, not the road. You helped me often enough in Latin class, now it's my turn."

They drove over the crest and the brake whistled as they descended the long incline; down below, one could already see the roofs of Bulach over the fruit trees. Machold held the reins short and kept his eyes on the road, while Knulp surrendered half contentedly to the pleasure of driving and to his friend's dictatorial hospitality. Tomorrow, he thought, or at worst the day after, I'll trundle along to Gerbersau if my bones still hold together. He wasn't a young whippersnapper any more who can afford to squander his days and years. He was a sick old man, and his last remaining wish was to see his home town again before the end.

In Bulach his friend took him into the big room and gave him milk and bread and ham. They chatted together and slowly recaptured their old intimacy. Only then did the doctor begin his examination, which the patient tolerated good-naturedly, with a touch of mockery.

"Tell me," said Machold when he had finished, "do you know what you've got?" He said it lightly, without solemnity, and Knulp was grateful to him for that.

"Yes, Machold, I know. It's consumption, and I know I can't last long."

"Oh, you never can tell. You've just got to get it through your head that you need a bed and care. For the present you can stay here with me; later on I'll find you a place in the nearest hospital. You've got crazy ideas, my boy; you'll have to get some sense into you if you want to pull through."

Knulp put his jacket on and turned to the doctor with a roguish look on his haggard gray face. "Machold," he said good-naturedly, "you're going to a lot of trouble on my account. It's kind of you. But it's too late. You mustn't expect too much of me."

"That remains to be seen. Right now you're going to sit in the sun, as long as it's shining in the garden. Lina will make up the bed in the guest room. We've got to keep an eye on you, Knulp. When a man who's spent his whole life in the sun and fresh air gets lung trouble, of all things, there must be something wrong."

With that he left his friend.

Lina, the housekeeper, wasn't pleased; the idea of letting a common tramp into the guest room! But the doctor cut her off short.

"That'll do, Lina. The man hasn't long to live, let's just make him comfortable for a little while. He's always been clean, and we'll see that he takes a bath before he goes to bed. Lay one of my night shirts out for him, and maybe you could give him my winter slippers. And don't forget that he's a friend of mine."

Knulp had slept eleven hours and dozed away the foggy morning. It was some time before he remembered where he was. When the sun came out, Machold had let him get up, and now, after lunch, they were sitting on the sunny terrace over a glass of red wine. The good meal and his half glass of wine had made Knulp lively and talkative. The doctor was taking an hour off from his work, to chat with his strange old friend and perhaps learn a thing or two about his extraordinary life.

"So all in all," he said with a smile, "you're satisfied with the life you've led. That makes it all right. Otherwise I'd be tempted to say that you might have made more of yourself. You wouldn't have had to become a pastor or a schoolteacher, you could have been a naturalist or a poet. I don't know to what extent you've developed your talents or made use of them, but if you have made any use of them it's been entirely for your own benefit. Or am I wrong?"

Propping his chin with its sparse little beard in the hollow of his hand, Knulp watched the red reflections playing over the sun-bright tablecloth behind his wine glass.

"That's not quite true," he said slowly. "My talents,

as you call them, don't amount to much. I'm a pretty good whistler, I can play the accordion, and I make up a little poem now and then; I used to be a good runner and I wasn't a bad dancer. That's the sum of my talents. But I didn't enjoy them alone. Almost always there were friends about, or young girls or children. My little gifts gave them pleasure and sometimes they were thankful to me. Why ask for more? Can't we content ourselves with that?"

"Yes," said the doctor. "Indeed we can. But I've got one more thing to ask you. You attended Latin school up to the fifth class, I remember that distinctly, and you were a good student, though not exactly a paragon. And then one fine day you were gone. I heard you were at public school and that was the end of our friendship. In those days a Latin student simply didn't have a friend in public school. How did it come about? Later on, whenever someone mentioned you, I thought: If he'd stayed with us in Latin school, his whole life would have been different. So tell me: what happened? Were you sick of it? Couldn't your old man keep up the tuition? Or was it something else?"

The sick man clasped his glass in his brown, emaciated hand and raised it, but he did not drink. He peered through the wine at the green garden light and carefully set the glass down again. Then he closed his eyes in silence and lost himself in thought.

"Do you mind talking about it?" his friend asked. "There's no need to."

Knulp opened his eyes and gave Machold a long, searching look.

"No," he said, still hesitantly, "I believe there is a need. You see, I've never spoken of those things to anybody. But now maybe someone ought to know. It's only a child's story, but to me it was important, it's plagued me for years. Strange you should bring it up!"

"Why?"

"Because it's been on my mind lately, and that's why I'm on my way to Gerbersau."

"In that case, tell me about it."

"Do you remember, Machold? We were good friends then, anyway up to the third or fourth class. After that we saw less of each other. Quite a few times you whistled outside our house and I didn't answer."

"By God, that's right! I hadn't given it a thought for more than twenty years. What a memory you have! Go on."

"Now I can tell you what happened. Girls were to blame. I grew curious about them rather early. At a time when you still believed in the stork and the baby—well, I had a pretty fair idea what boys and girls do together. I couldn't think of anything else, and that's why I stopped playing Indians with you and my other friends."

"But you were only twelve!"

"Almost thirteen. I'm a year older than you. Once when I was sick in bed, a girl cousin came to stay with us. She was three or four years older than I, and she began to play around with me. When I was well again, I went to her room one night. I found out what a woman looks like, I was scared out of my wits and I ran away. After that I wouldn't speak to my cousin, I was disgusted and afraid of her. But she'd given me the idea and all I did after that was to chase after girls. Haasis the tanner had two daughters my age, and there were other girls from the neighborhood. We played hide-and-seek in the dark attics, and we giggled and tickled and did things in secret. Most of the time I was the only boy; now and then one of the girls let me braid her hair or gave me a kiss. We were all children, we didn't really know what was what, but it was all very loving, and when the girls went swimming I hid in the bushes and watched them. —Then one day a new girl turned up, she lived in the outskirts, her father worked in the knitting mill. Her name was Franziska and I liked her from the first."

The doctor interrupted him. "What was her father's name? Maybe I know her."

"I'm sorry, Machold, I'd rather not tell you. It has nothing to do with the story and I wouldn't want anyone to know this about her. —Well anyway, she was bigger and stronger than I. Sometimes we tumbled and wrestled together. When she squeezed me till it hurt, it made me feel dizzy and half drunk. I fell in love with her. She was two years older than I. She kept saying she meant to have a sweetheart soon and the only thing I wanted in all the world was for her sweetheart to be me. —One day she was sitting all by herself in the tanner's garden down by the river. Her feet were dangling in the water, she'd been bathing and all she had on was her shift. I went and sat down beside her. Suddenly I plucked up my courage and told her I wanted to be her sweetheart. But she gave me a pitying look out of her brown eyes and said: 'You're only a little boy in short pants. What do you know about loving?' I told her I knew all about it and if she wouldn't be my sweetheart I'd throw her in the river and myself with her. That roused her interest. She gave me a woman's look and said: 'Let's give it a try. Do you know how to kiss?' Yes, I said, and gave her a quick kiss on the lips. I thought that was all there was to it, but she grabbed my head and held it tight and kissed me for real like a woman till I couldn't see straight. 'You'd suit me all right, sonny. But it can't be done. I can't have a sweetheart that goes to Latin school. They don't turn out real men. I need a real man for my sweetheart, a mechanic or a workman; not a scholar. So it's not possible.' But she'd pulled me up on her lap, she was so firm and warm and good to hold in my arms that I couldn't dream of giving her up. So I promised Franziska that I'd leave Latin school and become a mechanic. She only laughed, but I wouldn't give in, and in the end she kissed me again and promised that once I'd left Latin school she'd be my sweetheart and I'd be very well off with her."

Knulp stopped, seized with a fit of coughing. His friend looked at him attentively, and for a time they were both silent. Then Knulp went on: "Well, now you know the story. Of course it didn't work out as quickly as I expected. My father boxed my ears when I told him I didn't want to go to Latin school any more. At first I didn't know what to do; more than once I thought of setting fire to our school. That was childish nonsense, but I was serious about my main idea. Finally I thought of a way out. I simply stopped being a good student. Don't you remember?"

"Yes, it comes back to me now. For a while you were kept in almost every day."

"That's right. I cut classes, I gave wrong answers, I didn't do my homework, I lost my copybooks. Every day I did something wrong, and in the end I began to enjoy it. I certainly gave the teachers a bad time. By then I'd really lost interest in Latin and all that. I've always been impulsive, you know. When I had some new enthusiasm, everything else in the world ceased to exist. That's how it had been with gymnastics, and then with trout fishing, and then with botany. And now it was the same way with girls. Until I'd sown my wild oats and had my experience, nothing else mattered. And it is pretty painful to sit in a schoolroom reciting conjugations when all you can really think about is what you saw the other day when the girls were bathing and you were spying on them. —Well, there you have it. The teachers may have guessed what was going on, they liked me and shut their eyes as long as possible. My plan would still have failed if I hadn't taken up with Franziska's brother. He was in the last class of public school, and he was no good; I learned a lot from him, and everything I learned was bad. In a few months I finally got what I wanted. My father gave me the licking of my life, but I'd been expelled from Latin school and I was in Franziska's brother's class."

"And the girl?" Machold asked. "What about her?"

"That was the worst of it. She never did get to be my sweetheart. When her brother started bringing me to their house, she stopped being so nice to me; she treated me as if I'd gone down in the world. After a couple of months at public school I got into the habit of sneaking out after dark. It was then that I discovered the truth. One night I was roaming around in the park. There were two lovers sitting on a bench and I stood there, as I did now and then, spying and listening. When I crept closer, I saw it was Franziska and a young mechanic. They took no notice of me, he had his arm around her neck and was holding a cigarette; her blouse was unbuttoned and, well, it was horrible. All my trouble had been for nothing."

Machold patted his friend on the back. "Hm. Maybe you were better off."

But Knulp shook his angular head strenuously.

"No, certainly not. I'd still give my right hand for it to have turned out differently. Don't say a word against Franziska, she wasn't to blame. If it had come out right, my first experience of love would have been a beautiful and happy one. Maybe that would have helped me to get used to public school and straighten things out with my father. Because, you see—what can I say?—since then I've had good friends and casual friends, and even girl friends; but I've never relied on anyone's word and I've never given my own. Never again. I've lived my life as I saw fit, I've had my share of freedom and good things, but I've always been alone."

He picked up his glass, carefully drained the last few drops of wine, and stood up.

"If you don't mind, I think I'll lie down again. I don't want to talk about it any more. And you must have things to do."

The doctor nodded. "Just one word. I'm going to write a letter now—to see if I can get you into a hospital. The idea may not appeal to you, but there's no other way. You're done for unless you get proper care very soon."

"What difference does it make?" cried Knulp with unaccustomed violence. "I'm done for in any case. Nothing can help now, you know that yourself. Why should I let myself be shut up?"

"Don't say that, Knulp. Be reasonable. What kind of a doctor would I be if I let you run around loose in your condition? We'll get you a bed in Oberstetten; I'll give you a letter. And next week I'll come and see how you're doing. That's a promise."

The tramp sank back into his chair; he seemed on the verge of tears and rubbed his hands as though they were cold. Then he turned to the doctor with a look of childlike supplication.

"Well," he said very softly. "If that's how it is, I've a great favor to ask of you. Don't be angry. It's not nice of me, you've done so much, you've even given me red wine. You've been too good. I don't deserve it. But . . ."

Machold tapped him reassuringly on the shoulder. "Don't be silly, old friend. Nobody's trying to force you. Out with it!"

"You won't be angry?"

"Of course not. Why should I be?"

"Then, Machold, I beg of you. It's a big favor. Don't send me to Oberstetten. If I must go to a hospital, I'd like it to be in Gerbersau. There people know me, I'll be at home. It's probably better for the poor relief too, I was born there, and besides . . ."

His eyes begged fervently, he was so agitated he could hardly speak.

He's feverish, Machold thought. And he said calmly: "If that's all you want, it's settled. Good idea! I'll write to Gerbersau. And now go and lie down, you've been talking too much."

He looked after the tramp as he shuffled into the house, and suddenly he remembered the summer when Knulp had taught him how to fish for trout. He thought of the handsome, passionate twelve-year-old boy and of his knowing, masterful manner toward his friends.

The next morning was foggy and Knulp spent the whole day in bed. The doctor brought him a few books but he scarcely touched them. He was listless and dejected, for now that he was living in comfort, with fine food and a soft bed, he felt more plainly than ever that the end was in sight.

If I lie here another few days, he thought, I'll never get up again. He no longer cared much about life, in the last few years the road had lost much of its charm for him. But he didn't want to die until he had seen Gerbersau again and taken his secret leave of so many things, of the river and the bridge, the marketplace and his father's old garden, and of Franziska as well. His later loves were forgotten, just as his long years of wandering had dwindled in his memory and lost their importance for him, while the mysterious days of his boyhood took on a new radiance and magic.

He examined the guest room closely; he had not lived so splendidly for years. With a knowing eye and sensitive fingers he studied the weave of the bed sheets, the soft, natural-wool blanket, the fine pillow slips. The hardwood floor interested him too, and on the wall the photograph of the Doges' palace, framed in glass mosaic.

Then he lay for a long while with open unseeing eyes, too tired to concern himself with anything but what was going on in his sick body. But suddenly he started up, leaned out of bed, and with hurried fingers picked up his boots, which he examined with expert care. They were in bad shape, but it was already October, they'd last until the first snow. Then everything would be over. It occurred to him that he might ask Machold for a pair of old shoes. No, that would arouse his suspicions; you don't need shoes in the hospital. He ran his fingers over the cracks in the uppers. If he rubbed them well with fat, they'd surely last another month. No need to worry. His old shoes would outlive him and still be giving good service when he himself had vanished from the roads.

He dropped the boots and tried to breathe deeply, but it hurt him and made him cough. Then he lay still and waited, taking short breaths, tortured by fear of giving out before he had satisfied his last wish.

He tried to think of death as he had done now and then, but that tired him and he dozed off. When he awoke an hour later, he felt fresh and calm as though he had slept for days. He thought of Machold and felt that he would like to leave him some token of his gratitude when he went away. He decided to write down one of his poems; the doctor had asked about them only the day before. But he couldn't remember any, or he didn't care for what he remembered. Looking out the window, he saw the fog in the woods nearby and stared into it until a thought came to him. From the drawer of his bedside table he removed the clean white paper with which it was lined, and wrote with a pencil stub he had picked up around the house.

The flowers must wither
When the fog comes,
And people must die
And go down to their graves.
People are flowers,
They too will come back
In the springtime.
And then they will never be sick again,
And all will be forgiven.

He stopped and read what he had written. It wasn't a real song, there were no rhymes, but everything he wanted to say was in it. He moistened the pencil with his tongue and wrote under it: "To Doctor Machold, from his grateful friend K."

Then he put the paper into the little drawer.

Next day the fog was still thicker, but the air was cold and brisk, it seemed likely that the sun would be out by noon. Machold came and informed him that a bed was available at the Gerbersau hospital and that he was expected. Then when Knulp had pleaded with him, the doctor let him get up.

"I'll hike over right after lunch," said Knulp. "It will take me four hours, maybe five."

"That's all you need!" Machold laughed. "No hiking for the present. If we don't find anything else, I'll drive you over in my carriage. I'll ask the mayor, he may be taking a load of fruit or potatoes to town. One day more or less won't matter."

The guest gave in. The mayor sent word that his hired man would be driving two calves to Gerbersau the next day, and it was decided that Knulp would ride along with him.

"But you could use a warmer coat," said Machold. "Could you wear one of mine, or would it be too big?"

Knulp had no objection, the coat was tried on and found satisfactory. But since the goods were of the best and the coat was in excellent condition, Knulp with his old childlike vanity decided at once to move the buttons. The doctor looked on with amusement and gave him a shirt collar to complete the picture.

That afternoon Knulp, in great secrecy, looked himself over in his new clothes. He cut such a fine figure that he regretted not having shaved recently. He didn't dare ask the housekeeper for the doctor's razor, but he knew the village blacksmith and went out to see what could be done in that quarter.

He soon found the smithy and went in, proffering the old journeyman's greeting: "A blacksmith from foreign parts requests employment."

The blacksmith studied him with a cold eye. "You're no blacksmith," he said. "You can't fool me."

"True enough!" Knulp laughed. "You've still got your eyesight. Funny you don't recognize me. Remember? I used to be a musician. Many a time you danced to my accordion on Saturday nights in Haierbach."

The blacksmith knitted his brows and went on filing for a few minutes. Then he led Knulp to the light and examined him.

"I've got it," he said with a short laugh. "You're Knulp. People get older when you haven't seen them in so long. What are you doing in Bulach? I can spare a tenner and a glass of cider."

"That's very kind of you, blacksmith, I appreciate it. But it's something else I want. Would you lend me your razor for a few minutes? I'm going dancing tonight."

The blacksmith threatened him with his forefinger.

"You old faker! The way you look, it seems to me, you can't be very keen on dancing."

Knulp tittered gaily.

"You notice everything. You should have been a magistrate. Well, yes, I'm going to the hospital tomorrow, Machold is sending me. Naturally I can't turn up with this mattress on my face. Give me your razor, you'll have it back in half an hour."

"Hm. Where are you going with it?"

"Over to the doctor's, I'm staying there. Can I have it?"

Knulp's story didn't sound quite credible. The blacksmith had his suspicions.

"You can have it. But it's no ordinary razor, you know, it's hollow-ground, genuine Solingen. I want to see it back."

"You will."

"Of course. —Say, that's a nice coat you've got on. You won't need it to shave in. I'll tell you what: take it off and leave it with me. When you come back with the razor, I'll give you your coat."

Knulp made a wry face. "All right. You're not exactly a prince. But it's a deal."

The blacksmith produced his razor, Knulp left his coat as a pledge, but he wouldn't let the grimy blacksmith touch it. Half an hour later he returned the Solingen razor, his unkempt beard was gone, and he looked very different.

"Now all you need is a flower behind your ear and you'll be ready to go courting," said the blacksmith admiringly.

But Knulp was no longer in a joking mood, he put his coat on, said a curt thank you, and left the smithy.

On the way home he met the doctor, who stopped him.

"Where have you been?" he asked in consternation. "And the looks of you! —Ah, you've shaved! What an overgrown baby you are!"

But he was pleased, and that evening Knulp had red wine again. The two schoolfriends celebrated their parting, both putting on a show of good cheer and repressing any sign of dejection.

Early in the morning the mayor's hired man drove up with the wagon. Two calves with quaking knees stood there in wooden cages, staring wide-eyed into the cold morning. The first frost lay over the meadows. Knulp was helped into the front seat beside the hired man and a blanket spread over his knees. The doctor pressed Knulp's hand and gave the hired man half a mark. As the wagon clanked away in the direction of the woods, the hired man lit his pipe and Knulp blinked sleepily into the cool, bright-blue morning.

Later on the sun came out and by noon it was pleasantly warm. The two of them in the front seat got along splendidly. When they reached Gerbersau, the hired man was determined to go out of his way and take Knulp to the hospital. But Knulp soon dissuaded him and they parted good friends on the edge of the town. Knulp stood by the roadside and looked after the wagon until it disappeared under the maple trees by the cattle market.

Then smiling he turned into a path, known only to natives, that wound its way between garden hedges. He was free again. In the hospital they could wait.

Once again the homecomer savored the light and air, the sounds and smells of his native town, and the exciting, appeasing feeling of being at home: the crush of peasants and townspeople at the cattle market, the sun-drenched shadows of brown chestnut trees, the dark autumn butterflies in funereal flight by the city wall, the sound of the market fountain with its four streams of water, the smell of wine and the hollow wooden hammering that issued from the cooper's vaulted doorway, the familiar street names, each one shrouded in a dense and restless swarm of memories. With his whole being the wanderer drank in the enchantment of home, of recognition, of memory, of comradeship with every street corner and every curbstone. All afternoon he roamed tirelessly from street to street, he listened to the knife grinders by the river, watched the turner through the windows of his workshop, read old familiar names on freshly painted signs. He dipped his hand into the market fountain, but to quench his thirst he waited till he had come to the little Abbot's Spring, which still gushed mysteriously, as in years gone by, from the lower story of an old old house and gurgled between the stone flags in the strangely clear half light of its springhouse. He stood for a long while by the river, leaning on the wooden rail and looking down at the dark, long-haired water weeds and the slim black fishes that hovered motionless over the floor of trembling pebbles. He stepped out on the old footbridge and when he came to the middle flexed his knees as he had done as a boy, in order to feel the gentle, elastic counterthrust of the wooden structure.

Without haste he went on, forgetting nothing, neither the linden tree and the small grass plot by the church nor the upper millpond, which had once been his favorite bathing place. He stopped outside the little house where his father had lived long ago, and for a time leaned his back gently against the old door. He went to the garden and looked over a loveless new wire fence into a newly laid-out vegetable patch —but the weathered stone steps and the squat round quince trees were still the same. Here, before his expulsion from Latin school, Knulp had lived the happiest days of his life; here he had known complete happiness and fulfillment, joys without bitterness, the sweetness of stolen cherries, the delight of tending his little garden and watching his flowers grow, the lovely gillyflowers, the merry bindweed, the tender velvet pansies. And the rabbit hutches and the workshop where he had built kites and made water pipes from hollow elder branches and mill wheels out of balls of string with pieces of shingle for paddles. He had known the cats on every one of these roofs, sampled the fruit in every garden roundabout, climbed every tree, and made himself green dream nests in their crowns. This bit of world belonged to him, he had known every inch of it and loved it; every bush and every slope had held meaning for him, had had its tales to tell; every rain or snowfall had spoken to him; the air and earth had lived in response to his dreams and desires. And even today, it seemed to Knulp, this world belonged to him as much as to any of the owners of these houses and gardens. Which of them could claim to prize it more highly or to find more memories in it?

Between the nearby roofs he could see a tall, sharp gable. In that narrow house Haasis the tanner had lived, and there Knulp's first tender whisperings with girls had put an end to the games and joys of his childhood. Many an evening, as he left that house and made his way home down the darkening street, intimations of love had stirred within him; it was there that he had undone the tanner's daughter's braids, and there that he had reeled under the fair Franziska's kisses. He would take a look around over there later in the evening, or perhaps next day. But now these recollections held little attraction for him, he would gladly have exchanged them all for the memory of a single hour of the time that had gone before—of his childhood.

For an hour or more he stood by the garden fence, looking in, and what he saw was not the new, strange garden which already looked very bare and autumnal with its young berry bushes. He saw his father's garden and his own little flower bed, the bears'-ears he had planted on Easter Sunday and the glassy balsamines, and little mounds of pebbles where he deposited the lizards that he caught over and over again, inconsolable that none would stay and become his pet, but always eager and full of hope when he had captured a new one. Today he would have given all the houses and gardens, all the flowers and lizards and birds in the world for a single one of the summer flowers that had put forth their precious petals—ever so slowly—in his little garden. And the old currant bushes, each one of which he remembered exactly. They were gone, they had not been eternal and indestructible, someone had dug them up and made a fire; wood and roots and withered leaves had burned all together, and no one had mourned for them.

Machold had often come to see him here. Now he was a doctor and a gentleman and drove around in a fly visiting sick people. Yes, he was still a good and upright man; but he too, even this sturdy, intelligent fellow: what was he compared to the candid, shy, eagerly affectionate boy he had been then? Here Knulp had shown him how to build cages for flies and towers of shingles for grasshoppers; he had been Machold's teacher and his older, cleverer, admired friend.

The neighbor's lilac tree had grown old; it was withered and covered with moss. The latticework garden house was a ruin. And whatever they built in its place could never be as beautiful and pleasant and right as it had been.

Night was falling and it was growing cold when Knulp left the overgrown garden path. From the new church steeple, which changed the face of the city, a new bell rang loud.

He crept through the gate of the tannery; it was after working hours and there was no one to be seen in the yard. Soundlessly he passed over the soft tanning floor, between the gaping pits where hides were steeping in caustic, and stopped at the low wall, beyond which the darkening river flowed between mossy-green rocks. That was where he had sat with Franziska late one afternoon, their bare feet splashing in the water.

If she hadn't made me wait in vain, thought Knulp, everything would have turned out differently. Even without Latin school and the university, I'd have had the strength and the will to make something of myself. How clear and simple life was! He had thrown himself away, he had lost interest in everything, and life, falling in with his feelings, had demanded nothing of him. He had lived as an outsider, an idler and onlooker, well liked in his young manhood, alone in his illness and advancing years.

Seized with weariness, he sat down on the wall, and the river murmured darkly in his thoughts. The light went on in a window above him, warning him that it was late and that he must not be found here. He slipped silently out of the tanning yard and through the gate, buttoned up his coat and thought of sleep. He had money that the doctor had given him, and after brief reflection he went to a lodging house. He could have gone to the Angel or the Swan, where he was known and would have found friends. But he was not in the mood.

There were many new sights in the town, and formerly every one of them would have interested him; now he wished to see nothing but what brought back the old times. Then when he learned that Franziska was dead, everything paled and it seemed to him that he had come here solely on her account. No, there was no point in roaming about the streets and pathways, where all those who knew him greeted him with cries of jocose commiseration. When he chanced to pass the health commissioner in one of the narrow streets, it suddenly occurred to him that the hospital people might send someone in search of him. He went to a bakery and bought two rolls, which he stuffed in his coat pockets. It was not yet noon when he left the city by a road leading into the mountains.

High above the town, at the last bend before the forest, a dust-covered man was sitting on a pile of rocks, pounding the gray-blue shell-lime to pieces with a long-handled hammer.

Knulp looked at him, called out a greeting, and stopped.

"*Grüss Gott*," said the man, and went on pounding without raising his head.

"Looks like the weather's due for a change," Knulp ventured.

"Could be," the stone-breaker grumbled, and looked up, dazzled by the bright light. "Where you heading for?"

"Rome, to see the Pope," said Knulp. "Is it far?"

"You won't get there today. If you stop every few steps and bother people when they're trying to work, you won't make it in a year."

"Maybe not. Well, I'm in no hurry, thank goodness. You're a hard worker, Andres Schaible."

The stone-breaker shaded his eyes with his hand and looked at the wayfarer.

"Hm, you know me," he said thoughtfully, "and I think I know you too. I've only got to remember the name."

"Suppose you ask the old landlord at the Crab.

We used to hang out there back in '90. But I guess he's dead."

"Has been for years. Ah, now I've got it. You're Knulp. Sit down a while. And, *grüss Gott*!"

Knulp sat down, he had climbed rapidly and his breath came hard. Now, looking down, he saw how lovely the little city was in the valley; the sparkling blue river, the red-brown jumble of roofs, and the little green islets of trees in between.

"You've got it good up here," he said, panting.

"It's all right. I can't complain. But what about you? Not the climber you used to be, eh? You're wheezing something awful, Knulp. Visiting the old town again?"

"That's right, Schaible. For the last time, I guess."

"What do you mean?"

"My lungs are shot. You wouldn't know a remedy?"

"If you'd stayed home, friend, and kept your nose to the grindstone; if you'd had a wife and children and a warm bed at night, maybe you'd be all right. But you remember the way I felt about it. Now it's too late. Is it as bad as all that?"

"I don't know. —Well, yes, I do know. It's downhill, Schaible, every day a little faster. Good thing I'm all alone in the world and no burden to anybody."

"Whichever way you take it. That's your business. But I'm sorry to hear it."

"No need to be. We've all got to die some day, it even comes to stone-breakers. Yes, old-timer, here we sit, and neither of us has much call for rejoicing. You had different plans for yourself once. Didn't you want to work for the railroad?"

"Oh, that's ancient history."

"And your children? Are they well?"

"As far as I know. Jakob's working."

"Really? The time passes. Well, I'll be going now."

"What's the hurry? After all these years. Look, Knulp. Can I help you? I haven't got much on me, maybe half a mark."

"You can use it yourself. Thanks all the same."

He wanted to say something more, but his chest ached wretchedly and he fell silent. The stone-breaker gave him a drink from his cider bottle. For a time they looked down at the town, the millrace flashed in the sunlight, a wagon drove slowly over the stone bridge, and below the weir a gaggle of white geese swam indolently to and fro.

"I'll be getting on," Knulp announced once more. "I'm rested now."

The stone-breaker sat deep in thought. He shook his head.

"You know," he said slowly, "you could have been something more than a poor tramp. It's a damn shame. I've never been a psalm singer, but I believe what it says in the Bible. You'd better be thinking about it too. You'll have to answer for yourself, and it won't be easy. You had gifts, more than a lot of other people, and you made no use of them. Don't be angry with me for saying so."

Knulp smiled; there was a glimmer of the old innocent mischief in his eyes. He gave Schaible a friendly tap on the shoulder and stood up.

"We'll see, Schaible. Maybe God won't ask me why I didn't get to be a judge. Maybe he'll just say: Back again, you old fool?—and give me an easy job minding children, or some such thing."

Andres Schaible shrugged his shoulders under his blue-and-white checked shirt.

"No use trying to be serious with you. You think God will just crack jokes when Knulp comes along."

"Not at all. —Or maybe he will."

"Don't talk like that."

They shook hands and the stone-breaker slipped Knulp a small coin that he had secretly dug out of his trousers pocket. And not wishing to spoil his old friend's pleasure, Knulp took it without protest.

He cast a last glance down into his native valley and nodded once more to Andres Schaible. Then, seized with a fit of coughing, he hurried off. He soon rounded the bend and vanished behind the woods.

Two weeks later, after a period of cold fog had given way to sunny days brightened by late bluebells and cool ripe blackberries, the winter suddenly set in.

First, three days of bitter cold; then, as the cold abated, a fast, heavy snowfall.

All this time Knulp had been circling aimlessly, never leaving his home ground; twice, hidden in the woods, he had seen Schaible, but he had not called out. He had too much to think about. In the course of his long, useless marches he had sunk deeper and deeper into the tangle of his botched life as into a clump of brambles, and still he had found no meaning or consolation. Then, feeling very sick and faint, he had thought of returning to Gerbersau and knocking at the door of the hospital. But when after days of being alone he saw the town down below, the sounds that rose up to him were alien and hostile, and he knew that the town was no longer his place. From time to time he bought a piece of bread in one of the villages, and there were plenty of hazelnuts. He spent the nights in woodcutters' cabins or in the fields, bedded in straw.

Now he was crossing back from Wolf Mountain through the snowstorm, tired and wasted but still on the move, trudging on, exploring every copse and clearing, as though to make the most of his last meager provision of days. Sick and tired as he was, his eyes and nose were still alert; peering and sniffing like a hunting dog, he registered every rise and fall in the ground, every breeze, every animal track, though he no longer had any aim in view. His will had left him and his legs moved of their own accord.

In his thoughts he was talking with God; for several days he had been with Him almost uninterruptedly. He was not afraid; he knew that God can do us no harm. They were talking about the futility of Knulp's life: how things might have been managed differently and why this and that had had to be as it was and not otherwise.

"That was the time," Knulp repeated over and over again. "When I was fourteen and Franziska failed me. Everything was still possible. And then something went to pieces inside me; from then on I was no good. —You should have let me die when I was fourteen. That was the big mistake. Then my life would have been as beautiful and perfect as a ripe apple."

But God smiled all the while, and sometimes his face disappeared in the driving snow.

"Come along, Knulp," he said reprovingly. "Think of your youth, that summer in the Odenwald and the times in Lächstetten. Didn't you dance like a deer, didn't you feel the joy of life in every bone? Didn't you sing and play the accordion till all the girls had tears in their eyes? Do you remember the Sundays in Bauerswil? And Henriette, your first sweetheart? Was all that nothing?"

Knulp thought back, and the joys of his youth flared up in their dark beauty like distant fires in the mountains; they had the heavy sweet fragrance of honey and wine and the deep rich sound of the warm night wind at the approach of spring. Dear Lord, how lovely it had been, how lovely in joy and sorrow, and what a pity if he had lost a single day of it!

"Yes," he admitted, "it was beautiful." Yet he felt tearful and cranky, like a tired child. "It was beautiful in those days. True, there was sadness even then, and sometimes a feeling of guilt. But it's true, those were good years. Surely few men have drunk so deeply or danced so grandly or known such nights of love as I did. But it should have ended then. Even in those days there was a drop of bitterness, I remember well, and after that there were never again such good times. No, never again."

God had vanished in a snow flurry. Knulp stopped for a moment to catch his breath and spit a drop or two of blood into the snow. And suddenly God was there to answer him.

"See here, Knulp, aren't you a bit ungrateful? You make me laugh with your forgetfulness. We've remembered the time when you were king of the dance floor, we've remembered your Henriette, and you've had to admit there was a point to all that, that those days were good and beautiful and brought you happiness. But, my dear fellow, if that's the way you feel about Henriette, you must have a thought or two for Lisabeth. Have you forgotten her entirely?"

And again a stretch of the past lay before Knulp's eyes like a distant mountain range. And though it was not quite so happy and carefree as the days that had gone before, it shone with a deeper fervor, with the quiet light of a woman smiling through tears. Long-forgotten days and hours rose from their graves. And in the midst of them stood Lisabeth with lovely sad eyes, holding her little boy in her arms.

"I've been a bad man!" he lamented. "After Lisabeth died, I had no right to go on living."

But God interrupted him. With a piercing look of his bright eyes, he said: "Enough of that, Knulp. You hurt Lisabeth very much, we can't change that, but you know perfectly well that the kindness and tenderness you gave her outweighed the harm, and that she was never angry with you for one moment. You childish fellow! Can't you see what it all means? Can't you see that you had to be a gadabout and a vagabond to bring people a bit of child's folly and child's laughter wherever you went? To make all sorts of people love you a little and tease you a little and be a little grateful to you?"

After a short silence Knulp admitted in a whisper: "Yes, come to think of it, you're right. But that was all in the old days, when I was young. Why didn't I learn a lesson from all that and make something of myself? There was still time."

The snow was no longer falling. Again Knulp stopped

to rest. He meant to shake the snow off his hat and clothes, but he didn't get around to it, he was tired and lost in thought. Now God was standing right before him, His wide-open eyes gleaming like the sun.

"Let well enough alone," said God. "What's the good of complaining? Don't you see that whatever happened was good and right, that nothing should have been any different? Would you really want to be a gentleman now, or a master craftsman with a wife and children, reading the paper by the fireside? Wouldn't you run away again this minute to sleep in the woods with the foxes and set traps for birds and catch lizards?"

Again Knulp started off, unaware that he was staggering with weariness. He felt much happier now and nodded gratefully to everything God said.

"Look," said God. "I wanted you the way you are and no different. You were a wanderer in my name and wherever you went you brought the settled folk a little homesickness for freedom. In my name, you did silly things and people scoffed at you; I myself was scoffed at in you and loved in you. You are my child and my brother and a part of me. There is nothing you have enjoyed and suffered that I have not enjoyed and suffered with you."

"Yes," said Knulp, nodding heavily. "Yes, that's true, and deep down I've always known it."

He lay resting in the snow. His weary limbs had grown light and his inflamed eyes smiled.

When he closed them to sleep a little, he still heard God's voice speaking and still looked into His bright eyes.

"So you've nothing more to complain about?" God's voiced asked.

"Nothing more," Knulp nodded with a shy laugh.

"And everything's all right? Everything is as it should be?"

"Yes," he nodded. "Everything is as it should be."

God's voice became softer. Now it sounded like his mother's voice, now like Henriette's, and now like the good, gentle voice of Lisabeth.

When Knulp opened his eyes again, the sun was shining. It dazzled him so that he quickly lowered his lids. He felt the snow lying heavy on his hands and wanted to shake it off, but the desire to sleep had grown stronger than any other desire.